Rose

and the Silver Ghost

The blackness took longer to settle into the mirror this time. But at last the glass clouded, like paint settling into clear water, and turned a murky black. Rose's shoulders tensed, sensing that something was approaching. The blackness seemed to be tunnelling back, heading away to some strange place. Now, the odd silvery mist that Rose had seen before was flowing towards them through the dark. As it came closer, Rose's breath caught in her throat, and she had to force herself to start breathing again. It was a figure…

ROSE
and the Silver Ghost

HOLLY WEBB

ORCHARD

ORCHARD BOOKS
338 Euston Road, London NW1 3BH
Orchard Books Australia
Level 17/207 Kent Street, Sydney, NSW 2000

First published in 2011 by Orchard Books

ISBN 978 1 40830 450 1

Text © Holly Webb 2011

5 7 9 10 8 6 4

Printed in the UK

Orchard Books is a division of Hachette Children's Books,
an Hachette UK company.

www.hachette.co.uk

For Jon

ONE

'And one, two, three, and one, two, three, and – twirl, girl!'

Rose sighed, and twirled obediently. The last time she had danced, it had been in a Venetian ballroom, lit by candles hanging in huge crystal wheels from the ceiling. She had been surrounded by masked society ladies, and by the music, which swept her around in a whirl of silvery chimes.

The thin tinkling of the piano couldn't send her feet circling like that Venetian orchestra had a few weeks before. And Bella refused to obey Miss Fell's strict instructions on the polite steps of the quadrille. She kept adding fancy footwork, and Miss Fell did not approve. Even the jauntiest tune was dismal when the piano stopped every four bars for the pianist to hiss with horror.

Rose half-closed her eyes, and remembered soft white fur gloves instead of Bella's thin, hot hands.

'Rose! Not you as well! *Chassé*! Oh, stop it, stop it, I cannot stand the pair of you any longer. Tell one of the maids I shall take tea and a piece of lavender shortbread in my room.' Miss Fell sprang up from the piano stool with a remarkable energy for one so elderly, and strode – as much as she ever did anything so unladylike – out of the room.

Rose sank onto a small gilt chair, and shook her head. 'Mrs Jones will have a fit. I'm practically certain there's no lavender shortbread in the kitchens. She'll have Sarah making holes in the plain kind with a pin, and sticking the lavender in.'

'You'd think Miss Fell would know that, as she's such a powerful magician,' Bella said thoughtfully, chasséing perfectly across the polished floorboards and subsiding onto the windowsill beside Rose's chair.

'You would, wouldn't you?' The two girls exchanged glances, and Rose cast her eyes down to the floor, smiling a little. A few short months before, she had been an orphanage brat. The first time she had met Bella, she had been laying the fire in the younger girl's bedroom. Rose had moved from the orphanage to be the lowliest maid in the house of Bella's father, Aloysius Fountain, a powerful magician who worked as an adviser to the king. But then Mr Fountain's apprentice, the insufferable Freddie, had discovered that Rose could do magic too, and everything had changed. Dancing lessons – however horrible – were a world away.

Miss Fell had been living in Mr Fountain's house with them ever since they had returned from Venice, where they'd travelled to defeat the crazed magician, Gossamer. She wasn't anything as humble as a governess, but she *had* taken over Bella's lessons, and had insisted that Rose attended too. She also taught Freddie for some subjects, but Freddie had taken to developing interesting illnesses when it was the day for etiquette and genealogy.

Mr Fountain had been intending to find a new governess for Bella anyway, as she had finally seen off Miss Anstruther, her long-suffering last governess, just before they left for Venice. Bella's magic was now starting to show – and she couldn't control it properly. Rose rather suspected that Bella didn't want to, as it was more fun that way. Unfortunately, her magic was also immensely strong.

No one had quite realised *how* strong until they landed at Dover, two weeks before. As Mr Fountain had predicted, the Venetian ship hardly stayed in port long enough for them to disembark. The captain seemed to have very little need of favourable winds, and the spell-laden sails filled and swelled despite the stillness in the air.

Rose and the others were left abandoned at the quayside, something which happened to Mr Fountain very rarely. It was terribly cold, and Rose felt desolate, looking at the grey water, and greyer sky. It was surely about to snow again, which would at least cover the dirty slush around their feet. Their adventure in Venice had been dangerous, and frightening, and almost fatal – but it had been exciting too, and home was dismal. Tattered recruiting posters were pasted up on every wall, and the war with the Talish Empire seemed to have grown nearer and more certain while they were away.

Bella had huddled against Rose, moaning, her hands snuggled inside her huge white fur muff, and her blue eyes enormous in her pinched, cold face. 'I want a carriage!' she whimpered. 'I'm frozen. Papa, summon a carriage. I want to go home!'

'I want, I want,' Freddie muttered. 'Don't worry, sir, I'll run to the inn and fetch one. Sit on that bollard, why don't you?' He ushered the master over to the iron bollard, worriedly eyeing the area of waistcoat where

10

Mr Fountain had been stabbed. Bill, one of the young servant boys, helped him to set Mr Fountain down. 'And don't let Bella work you into one of her tantrums. If anything's going to bring about a relapse, it'll be that.'

'Thank you, Frederick.' Mr Fountain sighed wearily. The cold seemed to affect his spirits in the same way it ruined Bella's.

'I'm not having a tantrum!' Bella smacked Freddie on the arm. 'I shan't be spoken of in that horrid way. Apologise! Papa, make him!'

'Bella, dear!' Miss Fell frowned haughtily. 'Ladylike manners, if you please.'

'I'm not a lady, I'm only eight, and I'm cold, and I want to go ho-oome!' The last word extended into an eerie wail, and Rose put her hands to her ears as they began to throb, pain pulsing through them with the wobble in Bella's voice.

There were startled cries from the deck of the ship anchored nearest to them, a tall clipper, as the masts started to shake, and the sailors fell to the deck wrapping their arms around their heads.

'Bella, stop it… Please…' Rose whispered. There was no chance that Bella would hear her. How was she doing it? She had always had a piercing scream – Miss Anstruther had left Mr Fountain's employ after Bella had made her ears bleed. But nothing like this.

A break in the dreadful battering of sound let her open her eyes, but it was only a catch in Bella's throat. The wailing would start again in moments. Rose's one horrified glance around showed her the others clutching their heads as she was. Bill was on the ground, pulling his jacket over his head, and Mr Fountain drooped limply on the bollard. Freddie was trying to hold him up, his head buried in the master's shoulder as he tried to protect his ears.

Bella's father! She was killing him! Rose took a determined step towards Bella, who seemed to have been affected by the sound herself. She was lying in the snow, curled into a little ball, still uttering that unearthly noise.

'Bella!' Rose pulled urgently at Bella's shoulder, then cried out herself. Taking even one hand away from her ears was agony. 'Bella, you have to stop! BELLA!' Suddenly angry, Rose resorted to Mrs Jones's remedy for hysterical housemaids, and smacked Bella round the face.

The screaming stopped rather abruptly, and Bella uncurled and looked up at Rose, her hand to her cheek. 'Did you *hit* me?'

Rose took a cautious step back. 'Yes,' she admitted, wondering if she ought to run. But Bella looked more confused than angry.

'Why?' she murmured, rubbing her cheek. Rose could see the red mark across Bella's pale skin, but she didn't feel guilty.

'Look!' she snarled, hauling Bella up. She wasn't frightened any more. Now she was furious. How could Bella not know what she'd done?

Bella sagged in her arms, and looked round at the others. Mr Fountain's cat, Gus, was slumped on the cobbles, his fur trailing in the dirty ice. As the girls watched, his tail flickered, and he licked a paw weakly.

'You did that, Bella!' Rose snapped. 'Because you had a stupid, selfish, little girl's tantrum. You can't do that any more.'

'But I didn't mean to…' Bella whispered weakly. Then she ran to stand in front of her father, laying a hand on his sleeve. Freddie was kneeling by him still, and there was a thin trickle of blood running down the boy's neck from his ear, staining his starched collar.

'Oh, Papa! I didn't mean to hurt you.' Bella glanced up at Rose, with wide blue eyes, the whites showing all around the blue. 'Did I do that to Freddie? The blood?'

Rose nodded, and saw the expression on Bella's face change. The fear shifting slightly into thoughtfulness. Perhaps even a little pride.

'Yes. And it's horrible!' Rose hissed.

Bella nodded guiltily.

'Please don't do that again,' Freddie muttered, shaking his head as though he felt dizzy. 'Sir? Sir? Are you all right?'

'Mmm. Tell me, Frederick. Dear boy. Was that Bella?'

Freddie hesitated, not sure whether he might send the master into heart failure by admitting that it had all been Bella's doing.

'Yes, then.' Mr Fountain sighed. 'I really should have found her a better governess.'

'She doesn't need a governess, she needs a cell!' Miss Fell swept across the snow towards them. Her hat was on crooked, and she seemed old, and angry.

Bella was trying hard to look innocent, as though it was all just an unfortunate misunderstanding, but no one seemed to be appreciating the careful fluttering of her eyelashes, and she lapsed into a sulk.

There was an ominous creaking sound from up above them. Rose looked up slowly, reluctantly, as though if she didn't look, it might not happen.

'The mast!' Freddie muttered, staring with her. 'She broke the mast! I don't believe it. Sir, we have to move, please, you have to get up!'

The foremast of the clipper, a solid lump of wood taller than a tree, was swaying above them. Bella's screaming had splintered it fatally.

 14

'The sailors…' Rose whispered. 'It'll hit them – they're all unconscious on the deck. We recovered faster, because we know magic. Bill's still collapsed too, look.'

'Don't just stand there gawping and whining, you silly girl,' Miss Fell snapped. 'Help. And you too, Isabella, since this is all down to your ridiculous behaviour. Frederick, see to your master. And the cat, and the servant boy.' She marched briskly towards the ship's gangplank, and swept up it, her damson-coloured pelisse trailing over the wood. The girls scurried after her.

'Why are we going towards it?' Bella whimpered. 'We should be going *away*…' But she subsided when Miss Fell and Rose turned remarkably similar glares on her.

Miss Fell threaded her way delicately between the unconscious sailors, pulling the skirts of her coat away from them. Bella and Rose trailed behind her, staring up at the hypnotic swaying of the mast. Rose felt herself drawn towards it, wondering which way it would fall.

'Put your hands on it,' Miss Fell commanded. 'Isabella, stop play-acting, this is your ridiculous spoilt-child mess.' She snatched Bella's hand, and pressed it against the dark wood. Rose followed, wincing as she

15

felt the tearing shudders running through the timber.

'It's going to fall on us,' she muttered. 'Bella, if I get squashed, I shall kill you.'

Bella sniggered, but stopped quickly when Miss Fell glared at her again.

'I don't work with wood.' Miss Fell sounded frustrated. She was gripping the wooden mast as if she was trying to push her fingertips into it, but it was iron-hard, cured by the salt sea-winds.

Rose pressed her fingers against the polished wood, feeling for a hold, but it was no good. She hissed crossly, and felt Miss Fell's eyes on her, just a moment's glance.

Ever since they had first met Miss Fell in Venice, she had been looking at Rose oddly, and she kept dropping strange little hints. She seemed convinced that Rose must belong to one of the old magical families. Bella was certain of this too. Rose kept finding Bella staring, her nose wrinkled in a delicate little frown, as though she were trying to catch a scent.

'I can't get inside the wood,' Rose told Miss Fell apologetically. 'It's too dead. The sails maybe? Could we do something to those?' The old magician gave a thoughtful little nod.

'Our magic is very similar, I think, Rose... Agh!'

With a shrieking crack, the mast suddenly listed to

one side, sending Bella careering into Rose. Rose fell back, but was hooked upwards by something seizing her coat collar. An invisible something, a spell that Miss Fell had conjured up to catch her. At the same time, the sixty-foot mast suddenly exploded – very gently – into a cloud of powdery dust.

Gaping, Rose steadied herself, and dragged Bella upright. 'I thought you said you didn't work with wood, ma'am?' she murmured admiringly, looking around the deck of the ship, now heaped with little drifts of sawdust.

Miss Fell's lips pursed in a dissatisfied expression. 'I don't. I dislike merely – *blasting* things. No finesse. No delicacy. So uncouth.'

Rose nodded, and brushed the dust off Bella's bonnet. It would be rather lovely, she thought, to know one's magic well enough to actually decide what sort of spell to use, rather than just having to grab whatever happened to be passing through one's head, as she seemed to. She shivered a little. She knew that Miss Fell was an incredibly strong magician – she had watched her heal Mr Fountain of a fatal stab wound, in their fight against the mad magician, Gossamer – but this was different. That solid slab of wood was simply *gone*, and the feathers on Miss Fell's bonnet hadn't even twitched. It was pure power, and now Rose had had time to think, it was frightening. So frightening that Rose wanted to be able to do it too.

'I think perhaps now we should make for an inn,' Miss Fell said, twitching dust out of the folds of her pelisse. 'Rather tiresome to have to explain to these good fellows why one of their masts has disappeared.'

'Woodworm? Very hungry weevils?' Bella suggested, but Miss Fell ignored her majestically.

As they reached the quay, Bill was stumbling up from the ground, but Gus was still stretched out in the dirt, his whiskers trembling.

Rose hurried down from the gangplank to pick him up, lovingly wiping the greyish slush from his fur with her handkerchief.

'That girl…is a menace…' Gus moaned. 'I'm *dirty*. I need to wash…'

'Can't you just glamour it away?' Rose suggested helpfully.

Gus rolled his blue and orange eyes at her in disgust. 'Don't be stupid, Rose. If I glamour myself sky-blue I'm still white underneath! The dirt would still be there. I can feel it! Ugh!'

'What did she do?' Bill's eyes were rolling, and he staggered as he tried to walk towards Rose. Bella's screams seemed to have left his ears ringing. 'Is she one of you lot properly now then? Mrs Jones'll give notice, she always swore she wouldn't stay when Miss Bella was bringing the house down round her ears.'

Rose put an arm round his shoulders to hold him still, and sighed. 'Mrs Jones was right about that. I think if Bella had gone on longer she could have toppled a house.' She shook her head disgustedly. 'And not a hair out of place, look at her! How did she find the one clean spot in the harbour to lie in?'

After Bella's screaming fit at Dover Harbour, Mr Fountain had been horrified. He had blamed himself for allowing Bella to run wild, instead of insisting she stayed at home in London with a proper governess. And then he had begged Miss Fell to take Bella on as her apprentice, in the same way he had taken Freddie into his house for training.

When he suggested this in their private parlour at the smart Dover inn, Rose thought Bella was about to have another fit of hysterics. She had turned an unearthly white, and seemed hardly able to speak. Despite her awful behaviour, she did love her father dearly, and clearly couldn't bear the thought of being parted from him. Mr Fountain didn't seem particularly happy about the idea either. His moustache was drooping, which made him look like a depressed walrus.

'Please…' Bella whispered.

Miss Fell, seated in the best armchair, her back ramrod straight, and her hands resting on her silver-headed cane, regarded Bella thoughtfully. 'She certainly needs to be taught,' she agreed, although Rose thought she sounded somewhat reluctant. 'But I do not think my household would be particularly suitable. My London residence has been shut up for some years, for a start. I shall be staying in a hotel while I engage new servants. All most unsettling. Not the place for a young girl.' But her eyes rested on Rose as she spoke.

Mr Fountain watched her, his eyes thoughtful. 'A hotel is a most soulless place,' he suggested delicately.

Miss Fell stared back at him, her sharp nose making her look hawk-like. She inclined her head, very, very slightly.

'Would you not be more comfortable if you came to stay with us?'

Freddie's head whipped round at this, and his eyes widened in horror. He'd had enough of Miss Fell's old-fashioned ideas on the upbringing of children and apprentices.

'How very gracious…' purred Miss Fell. 'And then, of course, I would not only be able to teach dear little Isabella, but also Rose. And even Frederick.' Her eyes

20

closed, for the merest fraction of a second, as she contemplated that thought.

But Rose was quite sure that this was what she had been intending all along. Miss Fell had descended on the Fountain house in a mass of expensive luggage. Of course, Mr Fountain had not thought to inform his housekeeper that he was bringing home a house-guest, he simply expected Miss Bridges to deal with the consequences. In fact, Rose mused, Bella's selfish habits were inherited from her father – he merely managed to make them seem rather less obnoxious by adding a great deal of charm. Perhaps it was just that rich people were all inconsiderate, having never known anything else? Rose wrinkled her nose thoughtfully.

Luckily, Miss Bridges and Miss Fell seemed to like one another. Rose suspected that actually Miss Bridges would have liked anybody who was prepared to educate Bella – or at least try. It also helped that Miss Fell had made a special visit to the kitchens, and had been so very gracious to Mrs Jones about the orange syllabub she served at the supper the first night, that the cook didn't give notice after all.

Although, if Miss Fell kept asking for lavender shortbread, it was possible that Mrs Jones might reconsider, of course.

Rose sighed, and shrugged the thoughts away. She

sometimes thought that she would never understand people who had been born with money. 'I'll go down to the kitchens. Wish me luck. If Mrs Jones is in one of her moods, I'll be having bread and dripping for supper, without the dripping.'

Luckily for Rose, when she reached the kitchen, Mrs Jones was hidden behind her newspaper, with a cup of tea at her side, sighing heavily. 'Dreadful. Dreadful,' she kept muttering, as she rustled the pages.

'Another murder?' Rose whispered to Bill, who was drinking his tea out of his saucer, as no one else was in the kitchen, and Mrs Jones couldn't see him from behind the paper.

Bill shook his head, and slurped. 'War,' he muttered, eyeing the edges of the newspaper.

'Oh…' Rose sighed. The war with Talis had escalated over the last few weeks, and they had arrived back to find London papered with still more recruiting posters, and columns of soldiers marching through the streets. They frightened Rose when she was out on errands. Somehow she seemed to see those bright uniforms splashed with mud, and other worse things. Then she would blink, and again the cloth was only red with dye. It made her feel sick.

What would happen if the Talish emperor did as everyone said he meant to, and there was an invasion?

Would there really be fighting in the streets? Rose kept telling herself that Mr Fountain and the other magicians would never let it happen. But the emperor had magicians of his own. Lord Venn had even worked for him for a while. The plot to steal Princess Jane had been a subtle ploy to gain the emperor's trust. Who was to say that another powerful magician wasn't directing the Talish forces now?

Rose stared at the words screaming from the cramped type of the paper. *Cannon. 7th Light infantry. Treaties dissolved. Undue provocation…*

Her new life in the Fountain house was so wonderfully precious, and the bands of soldiers seemed to be marching over it in their heavy black boots.

'Those Talish. Traitors!' The newspaper shook aggressively.

Rose crossed her fingers behind her back, and cooed, 'Mrs Jones… Would we by any chance happen to have lavender shortbread?'

Mrs Jones's eyebrows appeared over the top of the newspaper. 'That woman will be the death of me,' she sighed. 'There's a porcelain jar of dried lavender in the larder, Rose, fetch it for me, there's a dear. And next time,' she eyed Rose sternly, 'next time, try to encourage her to want something that you know I already have. Use that dratted magic stuff.' She gave a slight shudder as she said it, but Rose still stared at the cook over her shoulder as she went to the larder. Mrs Jones detested magic, and kept the kitchen doors sealed against it by some ancient rituals of her own, which Rose suspected were just as magical in their own way as Mr Fountain's spells. She usually pretended not to know that Rose could do magic too.

'Miss Fell would see straight through me, Mrs Jones,' Rose told her, as she came back with the solid blue-white jar. 'She can make spells with her little finger that I couldn't do if I tried with all of me for a week.'

Mrs Jones folded up her paper, and smoothed it out with little thumps of her fat hands, as though she was squashing away things she didn't want to see. 'She seems such a nice, proper lady,' she murmured, and pulled the lid off the lavender jar with a sharp jerk.

'Looks like nasty little dead beetles,' Bill said disgustedly, as he peered into the jar. 'And the smell! She's going to eat that stuff?'

'It's a lovely smell!' Rose said, glancing at him in surprise. It made her think of drawers full of clean, pressed linens. Miss Fell herself smelled of lavender, Rose realised. She probably kept bags of it to freshen her laces, but Rose couldn't help wondering if her fondness for lavender shortbread scented her from the inside out.

'How are we going to put the lavender in the biscuits?' Rose asked anxiously. She had forgotten it was Sarah the kitchen maid's afternoon out, and she wasn't sure she was up to inserting lavender into shortbread herself.

Mrs Jones sniffed. 'Lavender glacé icing. It may not be exactly what madam ordered, but she'll have to lump it. We can't all cheat.'

Rose gave a brisk nod. 'I only hope it puts her in a sweeter mood. She's supposed to be teaching us painting in watercolours later on, and after the dancing lesson we've just had...'

'You're good at pictures,' Bill pointed out, but Rose sighed.

'Not painting them. Mine just happen when I'm talking, and I don't mean them to. Sorry, Mrs Jones,' she added automatically. Mention of magic was not usually allowed in the kitchen either.

'Watercolours are very suitable for a young lady, Rose,' the cook told her approvingly as she whisked a bowlful of icing.

'I'm not a young lady,' Rose pointed out, pursing her lips.

'But you could be, dear. Most girls would bite your hand off for the chances you're getting. Latin, and all that. Mind you, we'll be lucky if we're not all speaking

25

Talish this time next year.'

'You can't say you aren't a young lady, anyway,' Bill put in, filching a fingerful of icing while Mrs Jones examined the lavender. 'You don't know.'

'Oh, don't you start,' Rose told him witheringly. 'You're like the girls at St Bridget's, all sure they're really little lost princesses.'

'But you might be!' Bill protested. 'All that… *strangeness* had to come from somewhere, didn't it?'

'It's just an accident,' Rose muttered. But she didn't sound sure. Before she came to work at Mr Fountain's house, Rose had spent so long in the orphanage refusing to imagine that she had a family, that she found it desperately hard to think about her history now. She wasn't sure she wanted to find the people who had thrown her away – for that was what they'd done. They hadn't even bothered to deliver her to the orphanage, simply abandoned her in a churchyard – in a fishbasket, to add insult to injury. Why would she ever want to know them?

'What are we to paint today?' Bella asked, rather unenthusiastically, swooshing her brush about in a water glass.

Miss Fell frowned. 'Isabella, dear. Don't splash. Today I have found a painting for you to copy.' She brought a pasteboard folder over to the schoolroom table, and untied the ribbons. The watercolour inside showed a large house, built of white marble, like some ancient temple, and surrounded by perfectly green gardens.

Rose's shoulders slumped a little. At least in their lessons before they had painted flowers, and one of the china ornaments from the drawing room. Copying another picture seemed so dull.

'Try to match the colours,' Miss Fell instructed them. 'See the delicacy of line? Light washes, girls, no heavy-handed brushstrokes.' She sighed, and gently stroked a finger down the paper.

Rose wondered why she kept the painting tucked away in a folder, instead of having it framed to go on her wall. It was clear that she loved it.

Rose dipped her brush into the water, and tried to enjoy watching the colour spread across the paper. But it all seemed so silly! She was no pampered little rich girl, being groomed for a society match. Why on earth was she bothering with this?

The answer was simple, of course. Because she wouldn't dare refuse, although she was rather hoping that Bella might do it for her.

But Bella was doodling happily in a mixture of green and pink streaks, the odd tree shape appearing here and there. Rose glanced over at Miss Fell, who was staring out of the schoolroom window at the square, twisting a lavender-scented handkerchief between her fingers.

Irritably, Rose sketched in the line of the colonnade along the front of the house. It formed a pretty terrace, where doubtless the daughters of the family were allowed to stroll. *Probably they went nowhere else,* Rose thought bitterly, *constrained in corsets so they could walk only a few steps among the peacocks. Perhaps she had been better off in an orphanage after all? But a magician's daughter wouldn't be so hemmed in,* she admitted, spying Bella now mixing paint directly into her paint water to make tornado-swirls. Delicate mists of colour sank through the water – until it turned an ugly purplish-brown. No one could stop Bella doing what she wanted.

And not me, either, she told herself, half-looking at the watercolour, and painting without thinking. A pattern grew under her fingers, coils and swirls and feathery shapes, and the peacocks stalked slowly through her thoughts.

'What is that?' A papery whisper pulled Rose out of the strange, dreamy state she'd been in, and she jerked, streaking red paint across her sketch. Miss Fell was standing over her, the handkerchief now pressed to her lips.

'Oh – I'm sorry, ma'am, I didn't mean to...' Then she tailed off, looking down at her painting. The house was still there, but the composition had changed entirely. Now a young girl was walking through the scene, heading away from them towards the house, a shawl trailing from her elbows. She had one hand stretched out, with a piece of bread to feed the peacocks, and they walked beside her, their tails trailing along the ground like her long shawl. The feathers seemed to grow into the intricate pattern of the fabric, as though she was wearing them too.

'That's – that's not in the picture,' Rose stammered.

Bella leaned over from her side of the table to examine Rose's work. 'How did you paint that?' she asked wide-eyed. 'Rose, last week your posy of snowdrops looked like tree trunks. And who is she?'

'How did you know her?' Miss Fell asked, her voice still strange. 'You can't have known her! What did you do?'

When Rose simply gaped at her, the old lady seized Rose's chin in her hand, and pulled her face around, turning it so she could look into Rose's eyes.

'I didn't! I didn't do anything! I was thinking, and not paying attention, it just happened. I don't think I painted it at all,' Rose added, shamefaced.

Miss Fell let go of her, and clutched the back of

a chair, as though she needed it to stay standing. Rose and Bella stared at her, wondering what on earth was wrong, and whether they should do anything. This wasn't like Miss Anstruther's fits of the vapours. Rose was sure she could see the old lady's bones as she clung to the chair, and she was trembling. 'Miss Fell?' she asked hesitantly. 'Ma'am? Should we fetch you a – a cordial? Or some smelling salts?'

'Useless quackery,' the old lady snapped, seeming to come to herself all of a sudden. 'Make sure that you wash those brushes properly, girls. I have a slight headache, and I shall be going to lie down.'

But she tottered from the room, actually leaning on her cane instead of using it as part of her harmless-old-lady disguise as she usually did, and as the door swung shut behind her, Bella raised her eyebrows at Rose. '*Slight headache*, my foot,' she pointed out.

Rose nodded, and picked up her sheet of watercolour paper. 'Who is this?' she asked, staring down at the girl in the picture, and tracing the interlocking pattern of the paisley shawl. 'I don't remember her. How could I? I can't see her face properly, but I'm sure I've never met her. There's something though…'

Bella frowned at the painting too. 'She isn't all that much older than us,' she pointed out.

Rose rolled her eyes without Bella seeing. Bella hated being the youngest in the house, and refused to admit that Rose was older than she was. Rose didn't actually know how old she was, but she was reasonably certain she was at least ten or eleven. Bella was only eight. But Bella was right – this girl was young. 'Perhaps fifteen or sixteen?' Rose suggested.

'She's got a tolerable figure,' Bella pronounced. 'But I don't think her hair is naturally that fair. Probably it's the same colour as yours, and she put lemon juice on it.'

'Or maybe I just painted it the wrong colour,' Rose said.

'Oh, don't be so silly,' Bella snapped. You only held the brush. This was a spell. Miss Fell knew it too, and more than she was saying.' Bella's eyes were fixed on the strange sideways portrait, as though she was willing the girl to turn around. 'It was something to do with you and that house – and her.'

TWO

'You mean, she really is still working? As a *servant*?' Miss Fell's fluting voice filled the word with horror.

'Well, yes.' Mr Fountain looked uncomfortable, glancing at Rose as though he hoped she might rescue him.

'In between her lessons?' Miss Fell went on, glaring at Rose. 'She is an apprentice, how can she possibly be a maid as well?'

'I'm used to working, ma'am,' Rose murmured.

'Be quiet, Rose.' Gus walked along the back of the chaise longue, and wafted his tail over her mouth. Rose tried to argue and found she couldn't – her mouth felt as though it had been stuffed with hair. She swiped at it, and glared angrily at Gus, but he only purred, his eyes smug. 'She is ridiculously stubborn, and I have been telling her for months that she can't be a magician's apprentice *and* a housemaid.'

Rose hadn't realised that Miss Fell thought she was an apprentice and nothing else. She had lain awake through the night, hearing the city bells tolling hour after hour, as she wondered and worried about the girl in her painting. Then she had dragged herself out of bed at six to lay the fires. She had been laying Miss Fell's bedroom fire, and had stupidly dropped the fire irons in the grate.

The clumsy crash of the irons had woken the old lady – who had been remarkably patient with the careless servant in front of her, until she discovered who it was. Miss Fell had swathed herself immediately in a lace-trimmed wrapper, and summoned Mr Fountain and a tea tray to the drawing room. Gus hadn't been summoned – he had arrived out of incurable nosiness.

When they had returned from Venice, Rose had been unsure what she was supposed to be. While they were away, she had very definitely been a young lady – she had danced at a palace ball, for a start. Little Venetian servant girls had lit the fire in her bedroom – and to her shame, she had even stayed asleep while they did it.

But back at Mr Fountain's house there had been the flurry of finding a room for Miss Fell, and dusting it, and hanging the curtains for the bed, and fussing until everything was perfect. So Rose had found herself putting away her beautiful silver lace dancing dress on a hook in the tiny bedroom up in the attics, feeling quite sure she would never wear it again. And then she had run down to the kitchens to soothe Mrs Jones's panic about how to produce a suitable supper for the master and his guest, when (she claimed) there was only a haddock in the house, and that was past its best.

How could she possibly refuse to help? As Rose stared at Miss Fell's disapproving face, she imagined a similar expression on her own, as she told Miss Bridges that she was not a servant now, and would not be ordered around. She hadn't joined the family at the supper – which wasn't haddock, of course, although Mrs Jones swore that she was ashamed to send it upstairs.

'But I *am* a maid,' she whispered. 'That's why I came here. Miss Bridges took me out of the orphanage, ma'am. I can't forget that.'

Miss Fell's eyes glinted like flints. 'You must. You are no longer a servant.' She stared thoughtfully at Rose. 'It's much easier to be a housemaid, isn't it, Rose?'

Rose gasped. She was willing to bet Miss Fell had

 34

never scrubbed steps, or blackleaded a grate. How on earth would she know? Did she think maids spent all their time gossiping in the kitchens?

'She's right.'

Rose flinched as Gus delicately pricked her hand with one extended claw. She glared at him. She much, much preferred him as a dance partner, she decided.

'It may be hard work, but someone is always telling you what to do. You have a list to run the errands, or you just do the same back-breaking chores every morning. You never have to think.' The silvery-white cat swiped his whiskers across her cheek affectionately. Their tips felt like tiny dancing feet. 'No difficult decisions to make. You can be lazy.'

Rose stared down at her lap, where her hands were tightly folded. Callused, dry-skinned hands, which Bella kept being rude about. But Rose couldn't stand the thought of raw chicken-skin gloves, however much Bella swore they would make her skin pretty and soft again. She stretched out her fingers, eyeing the roughened patches.

Was that what it was? That she didn't want to give up a life where she only had to follow orders? She had always had marked hands, for as long as she could remember, for she had worked at the orphanage – they all had, even the littlest ones could carry washing. Rose had been proud of working, and delighted with her wages. Mr Fountain had paid her the same allowance he gave Freddie, since she became an apprentice, but that didn't feel quite the same.

'Freddie always has dirty hands too,' Gus told her helpfully. 'Covered in ink, and who knows what else.'

Rose sighed. 'But who will do my work?' she asked miserably. 'Already they're stretched below stairs, with me having so many lessons.'

'Can your housekeeper not engage another maid?' Miss Fell asked. 'Or even two. Really, the house seems to be run on a skeleton staff as it is.'

Mr Fountain sighed. 'I suppose so. I dislike new people in the house. It feels different.' He twirled his moustache irritably around one finger. His magnificent scarlet brocade dressing gown clashed horribly with the mauve armchair he was sitting in, and he looked generally grumpy, and very tired. He was spending even longer than usual at the palace, dragged into meetings about military strategy, and war defences, and he hated it. 'I will speak to Miss Bridges.'

'What will I do, when I don't have lessons?' Rose's voice was small. 'I could help in the kitchens anyway, couldn't I?'

'Of course not!' snapped Miss Fell. 'I am trying to get you out of the kitchens, child. You should be in the schoolroom, or the workroom. Or you may sit in your own bedroom, of course. You should practise your sewing, that would be very suitable.'

Gus gave a short purring laugh. 'Sitting cross-legged on her bed like a tailor, ma'am? She sleeps in a garret. No chair and only a hook for her clothes.'

Miss Fell closed her eyes, and shuddered slightly. 'Of course. Well, there's no shortage of rooms. I will speak to Miss Bridges about this myself. Perhaps the room opposite mine?' She asked Mr Fountain out of courtesy, but it was plain that she expected him to do as he was told.

'But I like my room, the one I have now,' Rose faltered, aware that she was sounding stubborn and silly.

Miss Fell hardly glanced at her. 'You are a young lady, Rose. You are being educated. It's hardly appropriate for you to be living in an – an attic.'

Rose gulped back a sob. Her precious first maid's place had gone, and now her little room as well. It was all very well to say that she would have a proper bedroom now, one that suited her station in life, but that room had been the very first place that was hers. The first clothes that had been only ever hers hung on those hooks. Her eyelashes fluttered miserably. She supposed she would have to get rid of those too. In her strange, unhappy mood, she forgot how delighted she had been with the new dress from Venice, and smoothed her too-short dark wool dress lovingly over her knees.

Why was she so frightened by all this? It wasn't that she didn't want to be an apprentice. But it seemed so final, to give up her other life as a maid. It had been there waiting if everything went wrong, she supposed. She could go back to the kitchens, and the way things were before. Rose ground her teeth. The *safe* way things were before. Gus and Miss Fell were right, even though she hated to admit it.

But she really didn't see why she had to give up her little bedroom. 'I don't need to move, ma'am,' she protested politely. 'I'll practise my sewing in the schoolroom, I promise.'

Miss Fell's eyes skewered Rose like daggers. 'It is not appropriate!' she hissed. 'Not for a...' She stopped herself sharply, her bony, knobbled fingers clenching into her palms.

'A what?' Rose asked, confused. Somehow she could feel that Miss Fell had almost said something terribly important, and it was there, just waiting to be dragged into the open, if only she could catch hold of it. She stared hungrily at the old lady, but Miss Fell was sitting calmly, her hands folded around the old silver mirror that she carried in her reticule.

'For a young lady,' Miss Fell repeated, each word falling into the room, hard-edged.

Mr Fountain sighed, and nodded. 'I'm sorry, Rose.'

Rose wasn't sure whether he was apologising for not treating her like a proper apprentice before, or for letting Miss Fell turn her life upside down now. She suspected he wasn't sure either. She sniffed pathetically, and Gus clawed her again. 'Stop it,' he murmured. 'Such self-pity. Disgusting. Ask for a new dress, and stop being so feeble.'

'I shall speak to Miss Bridges after breakfast. A meal which *you* will eat in the dining room, Rose,' Miss Fell pronounced, and she processed regally out of the room.

'The room on the other side of my room?' Bella asked, whispering to Rose over her boiled egg.

Rose nodded. Exactly what she needed. Bella running in and out of her bedroom all the time. Bella had never seen Rose's attic room – she had probably never gone beyond where the stair carpets stopped, as servants didn't need carpet.

Rose smiled into her porridge, wondering whether Bella could possibly be a worse neighbour than Susan, the other housemaid, who couldn't stand her. But then her eyes filled with tears suddenly. She wouldn't miss

Susan, of course she wouldn't, the girl had spent weeks torturing her. It would be a pleasure never to see that sharp-featured, sulky face again. But it also meant that Rose wouldn't see Mrs Jones, or Sarah, or her dear friend Bill – or only in passing in the corridors, and they wouldn't be supposed to talk. That wasn't going to happen, Rose told herself. She jabbed her spoon into the porridge angrily, striking a ringing chime from the delicate porcelain.

Miss Fell looked up sharply. She had taken most of her meals in her room since she arrived, only attending occasional family dinners, and she hadn't realised that Rose's absence meant she was eating in the kitchens. This morning she had appeared promptly for breakfast, in severe plum-coloured silk, with an ivory walking stick. She meant to see that her instructions were being obeyed. She frowned disapprovingly at the lapse of manners, but perhaps the stiff set of Rose's shoulders discouraged her from commenting.

'Oh, *good*,' Bella murmured sweetly, and Rose shuddered. Bella sounded altogether too happy about the idea.

'It will be delightful for you, Isabella, to have Rose close by,' Miss Fell pronounced.

Freddie smirked, and trod on Rose's foot. 'Notice she says it that way round,' he muttered. 'Good luck.'

Rose kicked him in the ankle, hard, and went back to eating her porridge with an angelic expression that she had usefully learned from Bella.

It felt odd, eating at the long dining-room table. She had eaten with the family in Venice, but that was Abroad, where things were obviously different. Now she couldn't help feeling as though someone might shout at her for sitting down. She had personally polished the silver teapot that stood in front of her – it was a beast to polish, with all those fiddly little bits around the lid. She kept wanting to smack Freddie for reading a penny dreadful under the table – if he didn't pay attention, he was going to drop bacon grease on the cloth, and it was impossible to get grease stains out of linen.

But she was actually drinking out of a cup from the Meissen breakfast service, Rose reminded herself. The tablecloth wasn't for her to worry about any more. Her fingers felt like sausages around the cup's delicate handle.

Miss Fell finished the meagre triangle of toast which had been her breakfast, and stood up. 'Isabella and Rose, we will discuss etiquette, and the proper spells for managing a well-run household, at eleven o'clock sharp, in my room. I shall go and speak to Miss Bridges about your new accommodation, Rose.'

'Why does she want me to move rooms so much?' Rose murmered, half to herself as the last whisper of Miss Fell's silken train died away.

'Don't you want to?' Freddie asked, looking up from his comic in surprise. 'I mean, I could see why you'd want to stay as far away from Bella as possible, but the room you have now, it's more like a cupboard, Rose.'

'I know. And I suppose I'd like to have a bigger room, it's just odd.' Rose glanced over at Mr Fountain, but he was deep in a book, and appeared not to be listening. 'It feels odd. I – I liked being half-and-half. I'm not a lady, I can't see how I ever will be!'

Gus licked the last drops out of a bowl of cream. 'Miss Fell does seem fairly sure that you are, or should be, already,' he murmured thickly.

'She's very set on it,' Rose agreed in a gloomy voice. It hadn't taken any of them long to learn that whatever Miss Fell was set on tended to happen, rather fast.

'I wonder why?' Bella mused, licking egg yolk off a little silver spoon with the tip of her tongue. 'Why does she mind so much?' She flicked a curious sideways glance at Rose.

'She's just like that,' Freddie shrugged. 'She wants things her way, that's all.'

Bella shook her head. 'I don't think so.' She dug her spoon into the egg again, perfectly aware that almost everyone around the table was now staring at her, while she diligently scraped around, finding the last little bits.

'Oh, pick it up and lick it!' Gus snapped. 'What are you talking about? What do you know that we don't?' His whiskers quivered with irritation.

Bella smirked. 'I watch, that's all. I've seen how she looks at Rose. And there was the painting, of course...'

Freddie pushed his chair back with a screech. 'We all know Rose is the most talented apprentice magician ever. Let's not go over it again.' He stomped out, slamming the door loudly enough to shake Mr Fountain out of his book.

'More tea?' he asked vaguely, waving his cup at Rose.

Rose filled it, waited until the master was safely back in a world of his own, and then stared at Bella and Gus. 'What was that?' she demanded, jerking her head at the door.

'He's jealous.' Gus shrugged. 'You take to spells more easily than he does, or so he thinks. It's true that Miss Fell doesn't seem very interested in teaching him. He feels slighted.'

'It's only because he's a boy!' Rose sighed. 'She's like Miss Bridges. She only likes tidy people, and he's always knocking things over. He doesn't want her teaching him anyway; he's always trying to get out of her etiquette lessons.'

Gus snorted. 'Etiquette. He doesn't care about that. The woman is one of the most powerful magicians of the age! That's what Freddie wants, her secrets. He's an ambitious boy. And she's giving them to you instead.'

'Oh.' Rose sounded doubtful. Despite Miss Fell's obvious power, so far all their new mistress had done was criticise her embroidery – and practically collapse in a painting lesson. Rose did not feel that she was being taught secret, powerful spells. She raised one eyebrow at Bella, who looked equally unconvinced.

'I expect she'll get to that. Maybe we need to be able to sew properly first,' Bella sighed. 'But anyway, Rose, that wasn't what I meant at all. I mean, you may be good at spells, but you certainly aren't as good as I intend to be.' She smirked smugly. 'I think Miss Fell is interested in you for quite a different reason.'

She paused, clearly waited to be begged, but Rose wasn't in the mood. She was still turning over the strange news that Freddie was jealous of her talent. He had been impressed when she first used her magic, impressed and furious that he had been shown up by a servant, but Rose had thought that had worn off by now. 'Oh, stop being so silly, Bella. If you want to tell, tell. Otherwise I have to go and study that diagram of curtseys before our lesson.'

Bella pouted, but she couldn't resist. 'Oh, Rose, it's obvious. She knows who you are.'

She sat back, looking proud of herself, and took a delicate bite of toast. But she was peering sideways at Rose to see how she took the news.

Rose put her hands in her lap, wrapped around each other to stop them shaking. She had suspected as much, but it seemed so much more real when Bella said it out loud. 'Why wouldn't she just tell me?' she whispered.

'I don't know...' Bella said thoughtfully. 'Maybe she isn't quite sure? It would be cruel to tell you if she wasn't certain. Or perhaps she thinks you aren't ready to know. It might be such an awful truth that it would send you screaming mad.' Bella crunched more toast. 'Yes, it's probably that.'

'She has to tell me.' Rose sat up straighter. 'If she knows who I am, she's got no right to hide that from me! She has to tell!'

Gus sniggered. 'Remember what I said about one of the most powerful magicians of the age? I don't think she has to do anything.'

'Shut up, Gus.' Rose stared at Bella, her eyes narrowed. 'Exactly what did you see, to make you think she knows? Did she say something?'

Bella blinked, a little nervously. She hadn't seen Rose like this before, and she was frightening. 'She looks at you... Rose, she...she looks *like* you. Now, the way you're glaring at me, you look like her. I think you're a Fell. And she knows.'

Gus surged up from the pile of cushions on his chair, and picked his way swiftly through the breakfast things until he was nose to nose with Rose. 'A Fell. Well, goodness me. The child could have said something useful, for once. A Fell child, in an orphanage. That would be a surprise.' He sat down, wrapping his tail around himself thoughtfully, and still staring at Rose. 'Why would a child from one of the most feared and respected magical families in the world end up in an orphanage, Bella?'

'I don't know.' Bella shrugged. 'But you think I'm right, don't you?'

'Possibly. Possibly.' Gus purred with satisfaction. 'This really is turning out to be a most interesting day.'

'It isn't just an interesting thing to talk about over breakfast!' Rose hissed at him. 'This is important! How are we going to find out if we're right?'

'You could ask her,' Gus suggested.

Rose shuddered. 'No. She'd just give me one of her looks, and tell me my petticoat was showing. If it was that simple, she'd have told me already, wouldn't she?'

'I'm all out of ideas, then.' Gus yawned, deliberately widely. 'Time for a sleep, I think.'

'I'll help,' Bella suggested hopefully. 'Please, Rose. It was me that told you. Let me help.'

Rose nodded reluctantly. Bella was right. She was the one who had noticed. It wouldn't be fair to shut her out now. 'Can you think of anything?' she asked.

Bella frowned. 'Nothing very clever,' she admitted. 'But I wonder if we could search her room. There must be something in there. Old letters perhaps. Some clue to who you are.'

Rose swallowed, but her mouth still felt dry. She'd had a horrible feeling that Bella would say something like that.

'Hesitating to say it for the third time, but *one of the most powerful magicians of our age.* Hmm? I think not the best person to burgle.' Gus jumped off the dining table, hitting the polished floorboards with a solid thump, and strolled out of the door, his tail-tip whisking happily. Rose stared after him, wondering who he was going to tell.

'Simple persuasion spells can be very useful, but in general, servants and magic do not mix.' Miss Fell continued. She was sitting in a wing chair by the window of her room, where she taught Rose and Bella

47

most of their lessons. They were perched on footstools in front of her chair, trying to concentrate on the proper management of servants. Rose couldn't help feeling that she knew rather more about servants than Miss Fell ever would. Between that and trying to look for clues without Miss Fell noticing, she was finding the lesson hard to attend to. It didn't help that she had to keep elbowing Bella, who had no idea of discretion, and kept turning round to stare at anything that looked like it might be useful in their search.

For once, Miss Fell was not sitting bolt upright. She looked tired – which Rose couldn't help feeling was her fault. The old lady didn't usually come downstairs for breakfast, preferring to take a tray in her room. By accidentally waking her this morning, Rose had added several hours to her day.

As she tried to concentrate on the old lady's fluting voice, Rose wondered how old Miss Fell really was. Rose had had some experience of glamours, but she had no sense that Miss Fell was using one. She just was one of those people who always looked perfect, even in her nightgown. Even now, only the purple shadows under her eyes, and her slightly huddled position in the chair, showed that she was weary. She was holding her pretty silver-framed mirror in her gnarled hands again, and she stroked it as she talked, gently running her fingers around the delicate frame.

'Rose, dear, pay attention,' Miss Fell scolded. 'And don't frown like that, child! You will have wrinkles before you're twenty if you sit and scowl. Really, direct sunlight and excessive facial expressions – ' Rose had to think for a moment before she decided this probably meant smiling was outlawed as well – 'are the ruination of the complexion. Don't frown, and never let me see either of you in the sun without a parasol. Rose, you are *still* frowning! Here, dear, look.' She handed Rose the silver mirror. 'Just look at the creases between your eyebrows. Disastrous.'

Rose took the mirror with a strange little skip of frightened excitement inside, and smiled sadly at her own anxious face in the tarnished glass. She nodded obediently at Miss Fell, and tried hard to flatten out her forehead, but it seemed to want to crease.

It was as she was handing the mirror back that it happened. The face seemed to come sliding out of the frame, as though the glass had been pulled sideways. Rose thought it was her own reflection for a moment, and some strange fault in the old glass had twisted it about. She had seen what was called a haunted mirror in the magicians' supplies shop that she ran errands to for Mr Fountain. The younger Mr Sowerby had shown her one to make her jump at her reflection all stretched out. But this was more than just old glass. The face was hers, but not. It was her, but *older*, and how could that be, unless the glass had some strange glamour spell on it? There was something else dragging at the corners of her memory too, a certainty that she had seen this face somewhere else. Rose tore her eyes away from the girl staring back at her, and looked up at Miss Fell, her mouth open to ask. But the old lady hadn't noticed what had happened and was still lecturing Rose on the perils of scowling. She simply held out her hand for the mirror, and laid it back in her lap. She gave no sign that she expected Rose to have seen anything odd.

Which left Rose wondering, was she the only one who saw strange faces in that glass?

'What was it?' Bella demanded, a little while later. As soon as they had been dismissed by Miss Fell, she had hauled Rose along to her own bedroom, and practically shoved her into the windowseat. 'Come on, Rose! The mirror, what did it do?'

'Did you see it?' Rose asked her sharply.

'No!' Bella smacked a cushion crossly. 'I knew it, there was something. You went the strangest colour. What happened? Was it one of your strange pictures? Oh, was it something about the war? I saw a paper on

Papa's desk which said that the Talish are most definitely making plans to invade. It said one of their plans is to fly across in huge balloons, but I can't believe that's true.'

Rose shook her head. 'Nothing like that. Nothing – grand. It's only that I looked in the mirror and it wasn't my face looking back at me. I've seen odd things in mirrors before, but only when I was *supposed* to,' Rose muttered. 'When we were scrying to find out what had happened to Maisie, and I saw Miss Sparrow. I asked the mirror to tell me that time, though. This was something different. I think that face is always in the mirror.'

'Who was it? Was she pretty? Was it someone you knew? Oh, Rose, stop sitting there like a lemon and tell me!'

'Bella, I think it might have been...my mother,' Rose whispered.

Bella's mouth fell open, and for once, she was speechless. She stared at Rose, mouth and eyes circles of amazement.

Bella looks like the queen's Pekingese dog with her eyes like that, Rose thought vaguely. Her brain was behaving like a butterfly, flitting from thought to thought and back again, and refusing to stay on the important things. Until she'd told Bella, she'd hardly dared say it to herself, but she was almost sure that she was right.

Bella got over her amazement quickly, and moved on to curiosity. 'How do you know? Did she look like you? And was it just her face, or do you think she could see you back? Is she *inside* that mirror?' Bella wrinkled her nose in disgust.

Rose frowned. 'No. It was only her face. She didn't move, and her eyes didn't seem to see anyone. I only saw her for a moment, but she wasn't alive. Or anything like that. It was more as though she used to look into that mirror, and it kept the memory of her.'

'I don't see why Miss Fell would have a mirror with your mother in,' Bella objected. Then her eyes brightened with the excitement of scandal. 'Maybe it was your mother's mirror and Miss Fell stole it! We really have to find out about this properly, Rose, it's just so exciting.'

Rose sighed. She knew she probably couldn't discover the truth on her own, but she wished Bella wasn't quite so keen. This wasn't one of those silly novels full of castles and dungeons and beautiful heroines that Bella's governess, Miss Anstruther, used to hide in the schoolroom ink cupboard. Bella couldn't seem to see that it was real. And just because Rose hadn't fainted dead away – gracefully, of course – like one of the idiot girls in the books, it didn't mean she wasn't upset. She had just seen her mother. It couldn't be the first time she had ever seen her, but it *felt* like it. Everything had changed.

'I don't know what we're going to do,' Rose muttered. 'But Miss Fell isn't going to tell me, that's clear, or she would have done it by now. So I need to find out myself. I'm not giving up!' she told Bella sharply. But then her shoulders slumped. 'Though I might as well, since I can't think of anything. The mirror is the only we clue we have.'

'We don't have it,' Bella pointed out, and Rose clicked her tongue irritably.

'You know I meant…' She trailed off. 'What if we did?' Her voice was scared, and she looked at Bella wide-eyed.

'You want us to steal it?' Bella asked hopefully. 'But what about what Gus said?'

Rose folded her arms, her face grim. 'If Miss Fell is actually my long-lost relative, then she probably won't kill me. Probably. She might kill *you*.'

'No, because then she would have to deal with Papa, and he's one of the most powerful magicians of the age too,' Bella said sunnily.

Rose nodded. 'I suppose it's good that she's making me move rooms. It'll be easier to get into her room from this floor than it would be from the attics.'

'What shall we do with the mirror when we've got it?' Bella's eyes were sparkling. She'd skipped over the difficult bit as usual, Rose noticed. 'Because whatever we do, Rose, we'll have to do it quickly. Miss Fell's bound to see it's gone when she gets up. She always uses it to put her hairpins in, haven't you noticed? She always picks it up when she's putting the ones that have fallen out back in.'

Rose shivered. 'So we'll have to creep into her room twice, so we can put it back as well. And she wakes easily, I know she does. I woke her this morning, and I hardly clanged the fire irons at all.'

Bella smiled delightedly. 'I know a spell we can use to be quiet. I was reading one of those strange old books in the workroom, the one with the cover that looks like squashed lizard.'

'Ugh. I haven't touched that one,' Rose admitted. 'It looks so horrid, I always think it's going to be full of poisonings and disgusting things to do in graveyards at full moon. Is it?'

'Of course it isn't. Think, Rose. Anything like that would be on the high shelves in Papa's study.'

Rose blinked. She hadn't thought of it that way, but now she rather wished that Bella hadn't been so sure that her father did have that sort of book. She wondered how often he used them.

'It's actually a collection of useful spells you can make from everyday ingredients. Things that you can find round the house. We need the Silent Slippers spell.' Bella looked proud of herself, but she was also eyeing Rose sideways.

'What?'

'It *does* have some ingredients you won't like.' Bella edged back over the coverlet a little way, as though she didn't want to be too close to Rose. 'The slippers are mostly made of spell, but the magic's woven into something real – something very soft and quiet…'

Rose stared at her panickily. 'What, Bella? Please, you're giving me palpitations!'

'We have to harvest rather a lot of cobwebs,' Bella admitted.

'Oh.' Rose smiled in relief. 'No.'

'You can't just say no!'

'Yes, I can, because I just did. I won't do it, Bella, you know I can't bear spiders.'

'I don't know why on earth not. Honestly, I'm the one who was brought up to be a young lady, I'm supposed to be screeching on a chair while *you* catch the spiders in a jam jar, Rose!'

'Please don't.' Rose put her hand over her mouth. 'I shall be sick on your silk bedcover.'

'Really? Just because of jam jars?'

Rose watched Bella file this information away for future use. The huge blue eyes were clear and innocent again in seconds, and Bella smiled. 'Well, I shall do it then. But this is an extremely big favour, Rose, you'd better remember that.'

Rose nodded wearily. There was very little danger of Bella letting her forget.

THREE

Rose enlisted Bill to help Bella on her cobweb hunt. The maids spent a great deal of time making sure that the family's part of the house had not so much as a strand of a cobweb – Rose had always had to do this with a very long brush, and sometimes with her eyes closed. Somehow, if she couldn't see the possible spider, it wasn't there. Susan would brush them down with her fingers, but even the thought of it made Rose gag. That awful claggy, smooth stickiness – how could Susan stand it?

The spell called for 'several hanks of fresh cobweb' which Rose thought was remarkably inaccurate. How many was several? To find even one cobweb, though, they would have to go out to the stables in the mews at the back of the house. Bill escorted the girls politely through the kitchens, where all the staff stood frozen; watching them. Rose stared pleadingly at Mrs Jones. The news of her permanent promotion to young lady had travelled very swiftly, she realised. There was a small pile in the middle of the kitchen table – her workbasket, the pinafore Miss Bridges had made her to put over her uniform if she had to be presentable. All the things she had left below-stairs.

'I will have them sent up to your new room, Rose,' Miss Bridges said gently, and Rose nodded. Thank goodness no one had called her Miss. She might have cried.

Rose waited outside the tackroom, ignoring the stable boys sniggering at her, while Bella and Bill went hunting spiders. She stood there, shivering in the January cold, and trying not to nibble her nails while she worried about burgling Miss Fell's bedroom.

'I do like this spell.' Bella had suddenly appeared beside her, looking even smugger than usual.

Rose jumped, and the stable boys hooted with laughter. Had Bella done the spell already, to be able to move so quietly? Rose glanced down at her feet, but they looked perfectly normal.

Bella's hands, though, were draped with silver-grey web, and she wasn't even wearing gloves. She waved

58

them at Rose. 'I think I might try breeding spiders in the schoolroom, Rose, so we can always have a supply.'

Rose slapped her hands across her mouth and moaned.

'She's gone green!' one of the stable boys pointed out with interest.

'Find her a bowl, mate,' the other one advised Bill.

Bill's response was to grab Rose round the shoulders and run her back through the mews to the kitchens, and shove her in front of the scullery sink – where for once Sarah wasn't doing any washing up.

Rose leaned on the white china sink, her head swimming, and tried to stay on her feet. Even though she was a young lady now, she refused to faint.

'She did that on purpose,' she moaned to Bill, who was hovering anxiously next to her.

Bill shook his head. 'Nope. She's just excited about the spiders' webs and this clever spell thing. Sorry!' he added quickly, as Rose lurched towards the sink again.

'I don't think I'm actually going to be sick – but her hands – she was covered… Ugh…'

'I didn't mean to upset you, Rose.' Bella's voice was husky, and she sounded guilty.

'Don't show me them again,' Rose gasped, wheeling round so as not to see Bella by the scullery door.

'I won't, it's all right, I've hidden them in my

handkerchief. And I washed my hands in the horse trough. I'm sorry, I really am. I didn't think. I was pleased, because we'd got such a lot, and I was excited about the spell.'

Rose dared a look at Bella, and saw that she was staring at the stone floor, looking guilty.

'I wanted to help you. I was so pleased that it was going to work,' she whispered. 'Rose, are you going to be able to wear the spell slippers?'

Rose was silent for a moment, gulping. 'Will it still look like cobweb?' she asked.

'There isn't a picture in the book – we could ask them not to, I should think. Would it be all right if they were just a different colour? Would pink cobweb slippers make you sick?'

'I honestly don't know!' Rose half-laughed. Then she shook her head. 'They'll have to do. I won't give up over something so silly.'

'You could find a different spell, couldn't you?' Bill asked.

Bella sighed. 'I could only think of this one. We could try, but it might take weeks, and we can hardly ask Miss Fell if she happens to know a good spell for sneaking around, can we?'

Later that afternoon, the two girls sat on the floor of

Rose's new bedroom. It would have been easier to do the spell in the workroom, but Freddie was in there, and he was still sulking. But sitting on the floor wasn't a hardship. The rug they were curled up on was worth more than Rose's year's wage, she was fairly sure. In her old room, there was hardly enough floor space to open the door, let alone to put down a rug.

Rose had her eyes closed, as even with one of Bella's handkerchiefs over them, the cobwebs seemed to move and shimmer and crawl. 'Do you need me to do anything?' she muttered.

'No, I don't think so.' Bella sounded so excited. She had done very few spells so far, or at least, very few spells on purpose.

Rose sat tensely, and heard her riffling through the pages of the spell book, and then tapping the paper thoughtfully with a fingernail. All the sounds seemed clearer and louder now she couldn't see. There was a rustling of fine linen, and shivers crawled up Rose's spine, like the spiders she couldn't chase out of her mind.

Bella whispered and muttered to herself, and Rose heard only odd words. Even Bella's voice sounded spidery and soft. She was desperate to leap up and race out of the room, but she didn't dare disturb the spell. If it went wrong, who knew what would happen?

Spiders in slippers might invade her brand-new bedroom. The thought of cobwebs on the heavy plum velvet curtains made her feel sick.

'Put your foot out!' Bella told her sharply. 'Quickly, Rose, I can't hold it like this for long!'

Rose's eyes snapped open, without her meaning them to. She stared at her foot, pale in a knitted white cotton stocking, and forced herself to stretch it out towards Bella's hands.

What Bella was holding looked like a hair net, a pale pink silk one. It glistened, and Rose tried not to flinch as Bella draped it over her foot.

'Now the other one.'

Rose's feet felt light as thistledown – as light as cobweb. It looked like she was wearing delicate, jewelled, pink slippers – but they were only spider-silk, beaded with gobbets of Bella's magic. Bella must have put a hint of glamour spell in them too, to change the colour, and make them look like pretty shoes, if anyone should see. It was very clever, deceitful magic. Rose was beginning to think Bella took after her father.

'We won't make a sound while we're wearing them,' Bella told her proudly, twisting to admire her own feet. 'Aren't they *pretty*? I wonder how long they last.'

A soft paw reached out and gently batted the pale pink mesh. 'Pretty but fragile,' Gus commented. 'Only the one night, I should think.'

Rose stared at him sternly. 'I shut that door myself.'

'Did you?' Gus yawned, showing a mouthful of sparkling white needles. 'Really. How interesting. And this is relevant how, Rose, dear?'

'How did you get in? It's still shut. You can't walk through doors, can you?'

'No. Well, I could, but why bother, when there's a perfectly good chimney, and a flue system that links up the whole house?'

Rose and Bella turned round to stare at the fireplace. The fire was lit, only a small blaze, glowing gently, and sending out a pleasant warmth into the room.

Gus was now licking one of his front paws, smoothing it around his ears luxuriously, his eyes blissfully closed.

'Next time I'll just leave the door open,' Rose whispered. 'I mean it, Gus, please. Don't do that again.'

Gus opened one eye, the amber one, and leaned across to swipe his tongue over Rose's fingers. 'Dear little Rose.' He rubbed his paw around his ears one last time, and got up, stalking over to the fire. He stared into it, dangling his whiskers dangerously close to the glowing coals.

Bella jumped up, and made as if to grab him away from the fire, but he glared at her, and she hung back.

'You'll burn your whiskers,' she protested. 'Think how awful you'd look if you were all singed.'

Gus sighed. 'Neither of you have any faith in me.' Before they could stop him, he put one paw up on the grate, murmured, 'A lot of dust here, Rose. Most unsatisfactory work,' and leaped into the middle of the fire.

Bella shrieked, and Rose would have done the same, except she felt as though the air had been knocked out of her, and she had no breath to scream.

Gus sat there for a moment with the flames swirling around him, looking mildly bored. Then he strolled back out onto the hearth rug, where he examined his paws carefully. Rose peered at them too, but they looked exactly the same as before, the pads a delicate apricot pink.

'Can you teach us that?' Bella asked eagerly.

Gus smirked. 'When you've grown a tail, Bella, come back and ask again. Rose, you cannot keep me out with a door.'

Rose shook her head. 'I wasn't trying to. But – we're planning to do something you told us was stupid. We thought we should plan it out privately. Freddie's been fuming in the workroom since he stormed out at breakfast, and we can hardly use the schoolroom in case Miss Fell walks in on us.'

64

'So what are you after?' Gus sat down in between the two girls, his whiskers glittering with excitement.

'Her silver hand mirror. She has it with her most of the time, so we think we'll have to do it tonight,' Rose explained.

Gus leaned forward, his shoulders heaving so convulsively that Rose wondered if something was wrong.

'Are you coughing up a hairball?' Bella asked in disgust.

Gus glared at her. 'I was laughing,' he pointed out coldly, 'at you being so blindly stupid. Do you actually think you'll get away with it?'

'We haven't a choice, and Bella's made us these silence spell slippers. We're going, whatever you say about it,' Rose snapped.

'Oh good. Well, I shall come too, just for the amusement value.' He sprang onto the end of Rose's bed. 'Be quiet now, children. I shall need to sleep, if we're going gallivanting all night.' Then he curled himself into a perfect white ball, with his nose tucked under his tail, so that they couldn't see his eyes to argue with him.

'Oh!' Rose huffed crossly. 'He really is impossible. I didn't ask him to come!'

'But he'll probably be useful, if he can stop himself

from laughing at us,' Bella pointed out.

Gus's tail twitched, and they couldn't tell if he was laughing or cross, so they decided to finish plotting in Bella's room instead.

'I don't want to wear my nightgown,' Bella hissed. 'I was going to wear my black velvet dress, the one I had for Uncle Dolph's funeral. It's perfect for going burgling in.'

Rose flinched. 'Don't use that word.'

'Stealing? Trespassing? Looting?'

'Ssshhh!' Rose crammed her knuckles in her mouth and nibbled them. 'Don't go on about it, or I might back out, and it'd be an awful waste of a spell, wouldn't it.'

'If you back out I shall go without you,' Bella retorted. 'This is the most fun we've had since we came back from Venice.'

'I'm not. But Bella, please just wear your nightgown, then if she wakes up we can pretend to be sleepwalking.'

'Both of you at the same time?' Gus asked.

'Oh, don't you start!' Rose begged wearily. She was feeling terribly guilty at the thought of stealing a valuable mirror, and she had frightened herself quite enough already creeping along the dark corridor to

Bella's room. The difficult bit had been tiptoeing past the particularly forbidding door behind which Miss Fell was sleeping – or so they hoped. If she'd woken up in the middle of the night and decided to read for a while, they were lost. As she crept along, Rose had been convinced that the ornaments on the little tables in the alcoves were all staring at her, and one of the paintings had definitely sniggered.

'Or we could both have heard a suspicious and frightening noise.' Bella nodded, twisting her face into a scared-little-girl look, and wringing her hands together. 'Yes, I see.' She stroked the black velvet dress regretfully, but closed her wardrobe door. 'Shall we go, then?'

Rose smoothed the front of her nightgown nervously, and nodded. 'We should get on with it. Have you got the slippers?'

Bella produced them from under her pillow with a flourish. They sparkled invitingly, but they slid onto Rose's feet with a slightly sticky eagerness that made her shudder. Still, they worked – Bella tried leaping on the creaky board two feet to the right of her dressing table, and there wasn't a sound.

Rose picked up her candle, and the girls padded out into the corridor, with Gus sliding around their feet silently. They paused outside Miss Fell's door, and

67

stared at the handle uncertainly. Moonlight was shining through the tall window at the end of the corridor, gilding the brass doorknob so that it seemed to ripple and shimmer.

'Open it!' Gus purred gently, nudging Rose's leg. 'Go on!'

'What if she's still awake?' Rose hissed. 'She always says she hardly sleeps.'

Bella immediately assumed her scared face. 'Don't worry, Rose, I will cry. You know how good I am at it.'

Rose grasped the handle, and turned it, gently pushing the door open. Miss Fell's candle was extinguished, and a pitifully small figure lay under a mound of quilts in the huge bed. Without her corsets and huge silken skirts, she was a tiny old lady.

'Look!' Bella breathed. 'On her nightstand!'

Next to the bed, the mirror glimmered in the faint candlelight, and Rose stole closer to snatch it up. She paused, her fingers hovering over it, watching Miss Fell sleep, wheezing gently in a nest of lace-edged pillows. It all seemed too easy. What if the mirror was enchanted against theft? What if it screamed as soon as she picked it up?

Rose grasped the handle, waiting for the metal to bite her back, or some strange spell to fell her to the ground. She was almost disappointed when nothing happened. It was only a mirror, and it did nothing.

She grabbed it up, and whirled around in the spell-slippers, shooing Bella and Gus out of the room.

They rushed silently across the corridor, giggling and panting and throwing themselves into a heap on Bella's bed, as the pent-up nerves took over.

Eventually, Rose stopped shaking and laughing, and stared down at the mirror lying on Bella's pillow. It looked unhelpfully plain.

'Now we have the rest of the night to work out why it's so special,' she murmured.

FOUR

The mirror was very pretty, made of silver that had been polished so many times it was almost silky. It was oval, with a handle, and the silver frame had a pattern of roses moulded all around it, like a garland. Several of the roses were so worn away that they were more like shadows on the silver. Rose stroked the pattern, smiling. If she had been born the young lady that everyone now wanted her to be, she would have been given something like this. Perhaps with a brush that matched, specially chosen for a little Rose. But Miss Fell's name was Hepzibah, so that didn't quite fit.

'Look into it!' Gus hissed, peering over her arm. She had told him about the strange vision she'd had from the mirror before. 'You might see her again.'

Rose swallowed nervously, and held the mirror out in front of her. She had a right to be anxious, she told herself firmly. She might be about to find out a vital clue to the mystery of her abandonment. Within the next few minutes, she might even have a family.

But then she bit her lip, and stared determinedly into the slightly dull glass. That wasn't true. How could she ever have a family, whatever she found in the mirror? A proper family would never have left her in the first place. She might get relatives, but that was about it.

She had been expecting to see the same odd reflection, the older version of herself. Instead, her own face stared back at her, worried, and heavily shadowed by the flickering candles. Behind her in the mirror lurked a blue-eyed child, and a highly curious cat.

'I can't see anything strange,' Bella complained.

'It looks like any old glass,' Gus agreed, pushing his nose around Rose's elbow and gazing into the mirror. A well-groomed white face looked back at him, and he twitched his whiskers at himself admiringly. 'What did you do the first time, to make it show you its secret?'

'Nothing.' Rose shook her head. 'Really nothing. I saw myself at first, and I only caught a glimpse of her as I gave the mirror back. She just came sliding out of the frame towards me, somehow.'

'So she's in the back of the mirror,' Gus muttered, sniffing at it. 'I can't smell a secret catch, but it may be very well hidden.'

'What do you mean, she's in the back of it?' Rose's hands shook without her meaning them to. She didn't want the thing touching her if it had someone inside it.

'A lock of hair is all I meant,' Gus snapped. 'Or a letter. In a secret compartment. Something that holds a memory of the girl, and it made you see her. Stop being so fussy and feeble, Rose.'

'Oh!' Rose nodded in relief. 'Yes.' She had seen the locket that Mrs Jones wore all the time, tucked neatly under her apron, and every so often when they had stopped work for a cup of tea, she would draw it out and polish it on the corner of the apron. She had shown Rose how it opened with a tiny spring, and inside there was a woven piece of sadly faded light-brown hair. Baby Maria Rose's hair, the tiny daughter that Mrs Jones had lost to the cholera so many years ago. This mirror could well have something similar inside it. Perhaps that was why Miss Fell loved it so much? Because it held the memory of someone she had loved?

'The lock of hair could even have belonged to one of her suitors,' Bella suggested dreamily. 'He died before they could marry – how tragic!'

Rose raised an eyebrow at her. She sometimes

suspected that Bella had read quite a few of those books Miss Anstruther stashed in the ink cupboard.

Bella went pink. 'Well, it might be true!' she protested.

Gus was still sniffing at the mirror, and even licking at the rose garlands with the tip of his shocking pink tongue. 'I'm sure there's something inside,' he muttered. 'Lay the mirror on the bed, Rose.'

Rose laid it down obediently, and Gus crouched in front of it, his shoulders sticking up sharply, and his tail lashing from side to side. Eventually he extended one paw, and raked a claw around the edge of the glass. Then he sat back smugly and blew on the mirror.

'Tip it up,' he told Rose, and she did, rather gingerly, turning the handle of the mirror so that the glass faced the coverlet.

With a splintering chime, the mirror-glass fell out onto the bed. Rose gulped, and lifted the frame back up, unsure what she would see inside. Her sensible instincts told her it would be the bare metal of the back of the mirror, or perhaps a silken lining bedding down a lock of hair. But the dark, and the late hour, and the flickering candles were screaming that it would be something horrible, like a finger bone, or that some disgusting apparition was already clambering and seeping out onto Bella's bed.

In the event, it was something completely different. Hanging out of the mirror frame was a piece of paper, the thick expensive woven kind that Miss Fell had given them for their painting lessons. On it was a portrait, a watercolour, perhaps by the same hand as the sketch of the house that Miss Fell had set them to copy only yesterday.

'That's who I saw!' Rose squeaked, tugging it gently out of the frame. 'I'm sure it is.' She picked up the glass front of the mirror, and held it and the painting side by side, looking from one to the other.

'Uncanny…' Gus purred, dangling his whiskers over the painted face. 'You to the life. But five – maybe six years older? That hairstyle is out of date too.'

'I can see why you thought she was your mother,' Bella breathed. 'Is there anything written on the back?'

Rose turned the paper over with trembling fingers, and traced the faded pencil inscription.

*For my dearest Hepzibah, a portrait to remember
me by on our travels. With all my love,
Miranda Fell*

'Miranda Fell! *That's* Miranda Fell?' Bella squealed excitedly. 'Oh, of course. I should have known!'

'Why? What do you know about her?' Rose seized

Bella's wrist and shook her a little. 'Bella, don't tease me, who is she?'

'Ow! Shhh, stop it, Rose, do you want to wake everyone up?' Bella cradled her arm tenderly and glared. 'And don't shake me, I was about to tell you.'

'Please, Bella,' Rose begged her, stroking the painted face. 'I want to know.'

Bella put her own hand over Rose's and traced the line of the face. 'You know who the Fells are, don't you?'

'Gus said this morning that they were one of the most powerful magical families in the world.'

'They were once,' Gus put in reprovingly. 'Sadly lacking now, of course. Living on their past glories, I should say.'

'Well, yes, that's what I'm about to tell her! Don't interrupt, Gus!' Bella glared. 'Miranda Fell was the only daughter of the family, the only child even. The heir. All the money was to come to her, and that huge great house up in Derbyshire. She was incredibly beautiful, so they say –' Bella looked critically at the painting, and then at Rose – 'and wonderfully strong at magic. She had everything she could ever want.' Bella glanced between Rose and Gus, her eyes sparkling. 'But she threw it all away! She disappeared, and apparently she ran off with the gardener's boy. Or

75

at least, he disappeared too, so one can't help but come to conclusions.'

'Of course one can't,' Gus muttered. 'Ran away with the gardener's boy. What a lot of nonsense.'

'It isn't!' Bella glared at him in outrage. 'It's what everyone says happened! My aunts still talk about it, it was the most enormous scandal.'

'They talk about that sort of thing in front of *you*?' Gus wrinkled his white-furred muzzle in disgust.

Bella blushed, her cheeks staining the faintest pink. 'Of course not.' Then she shook her curls defensively, and scowled. 'But if I happened to be hidden behind the drawing-room sofa... No one ever tells me anything, I have to listen! I remember them talking about it, and they did say it was the garden boy.'

'Hmf. Whenever a young lady disappears, it's always the gardener. No imagination.' Gus swished his tail disapprovingly. 'I remember thinking so at the time.'

'When?' Rose whispered.

Bella and Gus stared at her, and Bella's eyes widened. Gus straightened his whiskers, as though he saw how important a question this was. He glanced at Bella, and Bella wrinkled her nose, and then they looked back at Rose, together.

'It was about eleven years ago, Rose child,' Gus murmured, and Bella nodded, twirling one of her golden curls around her finger.

'Where did they go? Did anyone ever say, in all the stories?' Rose stared down at the painted girl, so as not to see them exchanging worried looks over her head.

Bella nodded and swallowed. 'Her parents searched the whole country for her. They found the coachman from the stagecoach, and they paid all the passengers to talk. Miranda and the boy went to London, Rose. They came here.'

It all fitted. Like one of those strange jigsaw puzzles that Bella had in the schoolroom, maps and pictures all cut up. But there was a huge hole in the middle of the scene, and Bella hadn't any more pieces, not even hiding under her chair, or knocked behind a cupboard like they usually were.

'But then what happened?' Rose asked. 'Didn't her parents find out any more?'

Bella shook her head. 'They simply vanished. The Fells had enquiry agents all over London. But they never found even a sniff of them.'

'So we don't know if – if…' Rose trailed off. She couldn't say it, even now.

Gus nosed her cheek gently, his whiskers fizzing lovingly against her cheek. 'If they had a daughter, and lost her, dearest one?'

'Mm. Or left her.' Rose brushed the sleeve of her nightgown over her eyes.

'Something must have happened to make them leave you,' Bella protested. 'Or – well, they could be dead, Rose.' She looked up at Rose anxiously as she said it.

Rose nodded. She had always rather hoped her parents *were* dead, as that would mean that at least they hadn't given her away in a fishbasket. But the thought was dreadful now, when she felt as though she was chasing a trail at last, following the clues towards her birth. The image in the mirror had drawn her so much closer to that girl, Miranda Fell, who might have been her mother. It felt as though she must have died only a few days before, just slipping out of Rose's clutches.

'They probably are dead,' she agreed quietly. 'But I still wish I knew how it had all happened.' She gave a bitter little laugh. 'I can't stop. Two days ago I didn't know anything, and now I'm getting greedy. Now that I've seen her.' Rose shook her head. 'And the gardener's boy. I can't feel the same about him, somehow, and it isn't fair.' She rubbed at the rough edge of the paper. 'I don't suppose there's a painting of him.'

Gus brushed his whiskers over the painting again. 'This painting obviously has a strong link to Miranda, or you'd never have seen her in the mirror. If we put it back in its hiding place, we could use the mirror to scry. To find out what happened. Then you might even see him, if we do it well enough.'

Rose looked doubtful. 'Would that work? I mean, the painting must have been done before Miranda ran away, mustn't it?'

Deep wrinkles of thought appeared above Gus's eyes, furrowing his white fur. 'Yes... But it might not make any difference. We have to hope so, anyway. And we need to be quick. Look.' He nodded towards the window. 'It isn't long till dawn.'

Rose glanced at the lightening sky. Very soon they would have to take the mirror back. This was their only chance. She slipped the painting back into its hiding place, and quickly, feeling silly but trying not to care, kissed her fingers and stroked them across that sweetly smiling face. Then she pressed the glass carefully back over the top, and gazed at her reflection. It looked just the same as before, perhaps a little more tired. Not like someone who might have a mother and a father now. Surely something so important should have made her look different?

'Rose.' Bella pulled her sleeve gently. 'Rose, come on, we haven't any time.'

The urgency had slipped into Bella's voice, even though she was trying to be patient, and Rose nodded apologetically – she had to stop thinking about things. But her middle-of-the-night mind kept worrying away with so many strange little thoughts. Would her mother like her new dress from Venice? Would her mother like *her*?

'Look into it properly,' Gus commanded. 'Rose, concentrate or I shall bite you, and a cat's mouth is a hotbed of dirt and disease.' He sounded quite proud about that. He nudged the mirror up in front of her face with his nose, and then peered into it hopefully with her.

Rose cupped her hands around the back of the mirror, and balanced it on her knees, cradling it carefully. Bella scrambled up on the bed next to her, and pulled the eiderdown around their shoulders, so that they sat huddled together, staring into the tiny circle of glass.

It was dark – but surely darker than it should have been? It wasn't only flat, reflected night, it was the dark that comes before a vision, and Rose felt her heartbeat start to race.

A faint mist appeared in the darkness, threading its way towards them from the back of the mirror – wherever that was. It felt so odd. Rose knew that she was holding it, and she could feel the edges of the moulding pressing into her fingers. But there was

80

a dark tunnel in the mirror, extending back miles. It made her feel dizzy looking at it, as though she were floating off down that black path, through the backs of her own hands, and somewhere out past Bella's bedroom wall.

'Rose! ROSE!'

'What? I'm doing it, you wanted me to look and I am, can't you see?' Rose muttered, narrowing her eyes and trying to see what that strange mist meant.

There was a frightened little moan, and Bella put her hand across the glass, severing Rose's link with the mirror.

'What did you do that for?' Rose hissed. 'I had something!'

'Did you indeed?' a cold voice enquired. 'Something other than the mirror you stole from my room?'

Rose finally looked away from the glass, and swallowed. Miss Fell was standing at the end of the bed, looking somehow taller than usual, as though fury had inflated her.

'Oh.' Rose ran her fingers over the back of the mirror, hating the thought of giving it back. 'We're sorry,' she murmured, unsure what else to say. Sorry was no good anyway when her hands wouldn't let go of the mirror.

'You stole,' Miss Fell repeated, her voice splintery cold.

'We – we didn't really want to,' Rose gabbled. 'But we couldn't think of any other way to find out, and…' She trailed off into silence. There *was* no excuse.

'To find out what?'

Rose swallowed again. Her mouth felt dry and sticky. How could she ask Miss Fell if they were related, when she had just stolen from her?

'It was you, Isabella, wasn't it? Passing on little secrets? Whispering?' Miss Fell seemed to glide as she came closer, and Bella shrank back against Rose, her eyes dark with fear.

'I didn't mean to – I only told her – I thought she ought to know! She looks so like you, and you kept watching her… What are you going to do?' Bella's voice was squeaking, higher and higher, and Rose gasped as she realised what was about to happen. Bella was losing control, falling into hysterics, which meant she was going to scream.

The noise began as a keening wail. Bella's eyes were still fixed on Miss Fell, but Rose thought Bella hardly saw her, there was only blankness behind the blue, as though Bella had gone and hidden away inside her own head, shutting everyone out with that terrible screaming.

'Stop her!' Rose snarled at Miss Fell, as Bella trembled and fizzed in her arms. 'It's you that's making her do this, she's frightened. Tell her you won't hurt her, you're not angry! Oh, ow...'

'Too late, I think.' Gus's ears were laid back flat against his skull, and his whiskers were bristling.

Miss Fell's anger had subsided and the glassy look of fury had left her eyes. Now she looked slightly worried. Considering that she rarely allowed her emotions to show on her face at all, Rose reckoned this meant that she was actually very worried indeed.

'How did you stop her last time?' the old lady demanded, clicking her fingers in front of Bella's glazed eyes. Her shoulders were shaking with the effort, but she did not cover her ears.

Out of pride, and anger, Rose didn't cover hers either. She wanted to. She was desperate to wrap her arms around her head and screw her eyes tight shut, in case any more of the agonising sound crept in through her eyelids, but she didn't. Instead she held Bella tight, letting the eerie sound shake them together. It was like being buffeted by furious waves, those great walls of jade-green water that had slammed against the ship on their journey home.

'I hit her, but I don't think it would work again, she's gone further this time. She isn't really there,' Rose gasped.

Miss Fell placed her hands gently on either side of

Bella's face, and peered at her. 'You're right. We have to bring her back to make her stop.'

The door slammed open just then, revealing Mr Fountain leaning on Freddie's shoulder, and looking horrified. Freddie had a striped scarf wound around his head, but it didn't seem to be working, he was sheet-white, and looked sickened.

'Bella! Bella, stop! What on earth has happened to her?' her father demanded. 'BELLA!'

Rose ignored him. The ebb and flow of the sound around her was still making her think of the sea-journey, and Freddie's greenish pallor had given her the merest hint of an idea.

She wrapped her arms even tighter around Bella, squeezing her close, and laid her face against Bella's, feeling the feverish heat of the little girl's skin. Rose closed her eyes, and let herself rock with the noise, riding it. The bed was a flimsy raft, and they were shipwrecked on the sound, dragged up to the top of each enormous wave and flung mercilessly back down.

She had never tried to use her moving pictures inside anyone else's head before, but if anything would break Bella out of her fit it would be this. She was dreadfully seasick, and had spent a large part of both their sea-journeys curled up moaning in her bunk. No one could scream and be sick at the same time, Rose was fairly sure.

Bella broke in mid-scream, the uncontrollable trembling giving way to coughs, and splutters, and a horrified whimper.

'Get a bowl!' Gus growled at Miss Fell, who was watching fixedly, the back of her hand pressed to her lips. 'Oh, Rose, stop it, you have me doing it too!' And he slunk over the side of the bed, and underneath, and could be heard coughing wretchedly into the chamber pot.

Miss Fell thrust a bowl of scented rose petals in front of Bella, and retired to a safe distance, looking pale. 'A most effective hallucination,' she murmured, sinking onto a chair.

Bella moaned weakly, and looked around her bedroom. 'We were out at sea,' she muttered. 'Why is everyone here?' Then she pressed her hand guiltily against her mouth. 'Oh! The mirror. Did I scream?'

'You did indeed,' her father told her grimly. 'I must go and reassure the servants. Thank you, Freddie, I can walk now.' He wrapped his dressing gown around himself tightly, glared at Bella, and stalked out of the room.

Bella stared after him miserably, so much unhappiness floating out of her that even Freddie was

85

moved to sit down on the bed and pat her hand. 'What happened?' he muttered.

'The girls have stolen a mirror from my room, Frederick.' Miss Fell's voice had lost the coldness, but Freddie still gaped at her, and then swung round to stare at Rose and Bella. 'Are you two mad?'

'Indeed.' Miss Fell sighed. 'No. I am being unfair. Presumably, Rose, you felt you had no other choice.'

'What?' Freddie muttered, looking cross. 'I shouldn't get into a miff with you two. I miss things.'

Bella managed a wan smirk, but Rose hardly even heard him. 'Will you tell us?' she whispered, her eyes fixed beseechingly on Miss Fell.

'I think I must.' Miss Fell gazed unseeingly at the curtained window. 'Yes. I think I must.'

FIVE

Miss Fell turned back to look at them at last. 'Give me the mirror, child,' she half-whispered. 'Please.'

Rose scrambled out from underneath Bella, and picked up the mirror, which she had dropped amongst the pillows. Shyly she padded across the rug and handed it to Miss Fell.

The old lady caught her wrist as she came close, pulling her gently towards her. 'Sit with me,' she begged, and Rose subsided onto the arm of the chair like a cloth doll. Miss Fell had the sort of voice that made one want to obey.

'I have to apologise.' Miss Fell still held Rose's hand, and she patted it gently as she spoke. Rose nodded politely, unsure how to answer. She could see Bella and

Freddie edging towards the side of Bella's bed, wanting to be closer, to hear what was about to happen. Even Gus came crawling out from under the trailing bedclothes, his whiskers drooping. He sat at Miss Fell's feet, washing furiously.

'How much have you worked out?' Miss Fell looked up at Rose, her dark eyes gentler than Rose had ever seen them.

'Bella…' Rose halted, unsure if Miss Fell would be angry again – she couldn't face another bout of Bella's hysterics.

'Isabella is a clever little girl,' Miss Fell said dryly. 'Too clever for her own good. You remembered the rumours about Miranda, didn't you?'

Bella nodded. 'And you do look alike…' she whispered. 'Just every so often.'

'I saw her picture in the mirror,' Rose explained. 'When you gave it to me to look at my frown lines. It wasn't me in the glass, but it was so like me. After that…we had to take it. Steal it, I mean,' she added shamefacedly. 'I had to know who she was.'

Miss Fell nodded. 'As anyone would, who had been left in such circumstances. Oh, dear Rose. I think Miranda must have been your mother. I can't know, of course. I never saw her again, after that strange day when she gave me the painting. If only she had said!

I would have helped. She never even sent word that she was safe. I suppose she was too afraid that the message would be traced.'

'She was your sister?' Rose's tongue seemed to fumble over the words.

'You flatter me, dear. My niece. Your mother was my brother's child. Miranda Fell.' She hooked a delicately pointed fingernail under the side of the glass, and pulled it out, revealing the painting. 'Yes, she is so very like you.'

'Did she run away with the gardener's boy?' Bella asked curiously. 'Gus told us that was nonsense, but Aunt Fay said she did.'

Miss Fell's eyebrows drew together haughtily. 'Your Aunt Fay, Isabella Fountain, is a gossip, and a hoyden, and gallivants with her footmen. And I'm quite certain that story wasn't meant for your ears, miss.' Then she nodded, very slightly. 'Unfortunately, in this instance, she had the story right. Except that he was one of the under-gardeners. A most handsome young man, and a good worker. John Garnet, he was called.'

'You didn't know?' Rose murmured. *John Garnet.* Her father. The name sounded…good. A solid, honest name.

'No. They must have been so careful. I suppose she knew even at the start that it would never have been

89

permitted. Oh, I knew something was different, and I suspected that she might be pining for someone, but I assumed it was one of the boys she had met in London – she had been presented for her first season, you see.'

Rose nodded, although she had very little idea what that really meant.

Miss Fell was staring at her again, searching her face. 'Seeing you in Venice, I told myself it was just a chance resemblance. Some strange quirk of nature. But then, when I heard your history, I couldn't help but wonder. Perhaps I should have said something then, but I wasn't sure, not at all. And you seemed contented, Rose, I wondered if you were better off without the truth – such as it is.'

'I wanted to be.' Rose picked at the lace cuff of her nightgown. 'I'd always thought I *was* happy not knowing, but the magic seemed to make everything different. I wanted to know where it had come from, all this strangeness.'

'When I gave you that painting of Fell Hall…' Miss Fell closed her eyes. 'It was a test. My curiosity got the better of me, Rose, I couldn't resist seeing what would happen. I thought almost certainly nothing. You had never been there, after all, why should you react? And then you painted her. Miranda loved those peacocks. She would wander up and down the lawn for hours, slipping them crumbs. She called that wrap her peacock shawl, and swore they were feather patterns.' She sighed. 'I still don't know how you did it.'

'I didn't,' Rose muttered. 'It just happened.'

'Unconscious magic can be the strongest of all. At any rate, it proved to me who you were. I shouldn't have reacted the way I did, but then I never went back, you see. I haven't been to Fell Hall in eleven years.'

'Why ever not?' Freddie demanded in surprise, and then looked guilty. 'Sorry, ma'am, I didn't mean…'

Miss Fell gave him a very small smile. 'I quarrelled with my brother, Frederick.' She patted Rose's hand again, but this time it felt almost like a warning. 'When your grandfather, my brother, found out that Miranda had run away with a servant, he disowned her. He changed his will, and left everything to a charity that provides meat for stray cats.'

Gus coughed appreciatively. Miss Fell nodded. 'Quite. But this was not in a spirit of generosity, or out of any love for your race, my dear. He was purely furious. He was ashamed that a daughter of his should have done such a thing, and then that she had the gall to hide so well that he couldn't find her and drag her back. I tried to dissuade him, and he made it very clear that Miranda would not be welcome there ever again, and that if I persisted in taking her side, neither would

91

I.' She sighed. 'And so I left. I had my own money, from my mother, so I came to live in London, and I travelled, and I looked for her wherever I went. I was almost grateful to Miranda, when I wasn't furious with her for disappearing without telling me. I had always longed to go abroad, but Fell Hall... Well, it has some strange magic of its own. Leaving it can be very difficult. Which only proves, Rose, how much your mother must have loved that boy.'

Rose nodded. 'I wish I knew what had happened. It must all have gone wrong.'

'Horribly wrong.' Miss Fell sighed. 'I had always hoped I might find her again, you know. Even that she might find me. But Miranda wasn't the sort of person to abandon a child, Rose. That's why it was so strange for me to see you – I was so excited to think that you might be Miranda's daughter. But at the same time, you were an orphan, and it meant that Miranda was dead, and somehow I'd never quite brought myself to believe that before. I was sure I would have known, or felt it somehow. Instead I'd always convinced myself that she was just living hidden away somewhere, and one day she would come back.'

'I'm sorry,' Rose murmured, feeling stricken.

'Oh, Rose! None of this is your fault – and I feel as if I have Miranda reincarnated, which is an amazing gift.'

She smiled, and stroked Rose's hair. 'Even your grandfather would have relented, seeing you, I think.'

'Would have?' Freddie asked, before Rose could. He was lying on Bella's bed now, with his chin on his hands, listening avidly, as if this were some exciting bedtime story.

'He died. A few years ago, and your grandmother too, Rose. I'm sorry. I'm afraid I must be your only close relative.'

'My – my great-aunt?' Rose stammered, hardly sure if she dared to suggest it.

'Yes.' Miss Fell smiled at her.

'So who lives at Fell Hall now?' Freddie asked, breaking into the strange little silence.

Miss Fell shook her head. 'No one. There was a huge fight about the inheritance. Some distant cousins objected to the cats' meat people, and contested the will. They thought they should have Fell Hall.' She gave a grim little smile. 'The court agreed that your grandfather had behaved out of spite, but the case didn't turn out the way they expected. I had been gone long enough that Cousin Magnus had forgotten I existed. The court ruled that the house belonged to me.'

'But you've still never been back?' Freddie gawped at her.

'Close your mouth, boy, you'll catch flies,' Miss Fell told him tartly.

Freddie shut his mouth with a snap, but he was still staring at her, and she sighed. 'I would always be thinking of Miranda. I didn't want to go back. I have a steward there, and he keeps the house with a skeleton staff, but I am afraid the old place is probably rather ramshackle now.'

Rose smiled to herself over Miss Fell's head. She was willing to bet that a skeleton staff meant at least twenty people, and ramshackle just that they weren't keeping all the silver polished.

'You should have this, Rose.' Miss Fell stroked the roses around the edge of the mirror, then closed her eyes for a second, and handed it quickly to Rose.

Rose held it, wide-eyed. 'It's yours…'

'It was your mother's first. I gave it to her, in fact. For her twelfth birthday, with a jewellery box to match. She loved it.'

'But didn't she take it with her? Could she not take anything at all?' Rose imagined her heading out into the night – somehow she was sure she had gone at night – with only the clothes she stood up in.

'They decided she must have had a small bag, but she couldn't pack properly, it would have been too obvious. And oddly enough, Rose, she did take this mirror with her. She left the jewellery box. That's in my room too, but you missed it on your little spying mission, my dears.' Miss Fell's eyes glinted as Rose tensed beside her, but then Rose saw that it was the brightness of tears. 'It was brought back to me, by a friend, who saw it in a jeweller's shop. He recognised the Fell emblem on the back, you see?' Miss Fell turned the mirror over in Rose's hands to show them, and Rose frowned. She hadn't noticed a crest or a coat of arms. But Miss Fell was pointing to the engraved rose garlands. Cleverly twisted into one of them was a tiny mouse, its tail wrapped around a rose stem, and the little sharp-eyed face peering out from between the thorns. 'The mouse in the roses is the sign of the Fells. Some strange dream that one of our ancestors had long ago, I think.'

Rose ran her finger over the little mouse, smiling. It seemed a more suitable emblem for her family than a proud lion, or a gryphon or some such fabled beast. She felt at home with a mouse.

'I knew that things must be very wrong, when he handed it to me.' Miss Fell's voice was threadlike. 'She wouldn't have given it up easily.' She struggled up out of the chair, looking suddenly exhausted. 'I am going back to bed. I would appreciate it, dear ones, if you could manage not to produce any more disasters until late morning. Perhaps even after lunch.'

Rose and Bella nodded guiltily, and then Rose suddenly had to strangle the most enormous yawn. Miss Fell had very strict ideas on young ladies yawning. One simply didn't.

'I am coming to sleep on your bed, Rose,' Gus announced. 'I approve of your new bedroom, very much, although I wouldn't personally have chosen that odd violet shade for the curtains. But in general a much more fitting place for me to sleep.' He wove himself around her ankles as she walked wearily to the door. 'I will guard the mirror for you, if you like. Or are you going to sleep holding it?' He stared up at her, his mismatched eyes bright and knowing, and Rose blushed scarlet.

'If ever I fight with you again, Rose, you must just remind me of all this,' Freddie muttered.

They were sitting in the workroom with a plate of toast that Rose had begged from Mrs Jones, since they had all slept through breakfast. Bella and Rose were explaining everything that had happened since they found the painting to Freddie. Gus was apparently asleep in front of the fire, but his tail twitched irritably every time he disagreed with the girls' storytelling.

'I can't believe you're a Fell.' Freddie shook his head.

'That's like magical royalty, Rose. One of the Fells back in Tudor times had a pet dragon, or so everyone says.'

There was a disgusted sniff from the hearthrug, and Freddie glared. 'They do say it! Just because you don't believe in dragons it doesn't mean I can't. And I do.'

'Stop talking fairy tales and do something useful with that mirror.' Gus stretched himself paw by paw as he uncoiled from the mat.

Rose blinked. She had the mirror on the table in front of her, at a safe distance from the toast. She hadn't wanted to leave it in her room. 'Such as what?'

'Scry in it, of course! Have you forgotten what you *borrowed* it for?'

'But we don't need to now, Miss Fell told us about my mother.' Rose frowned at Gus, who had jumped on to the table and was sniffing thoughtfully at the mirror again.

'You did start to see something in it.' Bella, who had been playing idly with a crust of toast, sat up straight, her eyes eager. 'You said so, while Miss Fell was being so frightening. In fact, it was interesting enough that you didn't even notice her.'

Rose nodded. 'A strange black tunnel. I think there was someone about to come out of it.' She shuddered. 'Or something, perhaps. It could have been anything.'

'If we all do it together we're even more likely to

make it work,' Freddie suggested, fingering the silver roses. 'Don't you think?'

'Let Rose hold it,' Gus told him. 'She is the one with the family connection. You and Bella can hold *her*, and lend her the strength of your magic.'

Rose nodded. Family connection, Gus had said. It made her heart jitter in a strange way. It wasn't family in the sense she had thought of it – it was more like history. A very distant relative with a pet dragon. A link to a family house. Even if it was all about to fall down because her grandfather had been so furious with her mother. 'I still don't know what we're actually looking for,' she said, sounding rather dazed.

'A glimpse into the past,' Gus suggested. 'We want to know what happened.'

'This mirror was your mother's, so maybe we can scry for her.' Bella sounded a little hesitant.

'*Can* you scry for ghosts?' Freddie asked Gus.

'Freddie! I was trying to be tactful!' Bella scolded.

'Everyone is so sure she's dead,' Rose murmured, stroking the mirror.

There was a silence, which no one wanted to break. Eventually Gus nudged her hand with his muzzle. It felt whisker-bristly. 'You heard your great-aunt. She sounded quite sure.'

'I know. I know she must be dead.' Rose smiled,

biting her lip, and then looked away from them all. 'I know it's stupid. I'm chasing rainbows, wanting her still to be alive. It just seems so unfair, that we've found out all about her, and I can't even talk to her. Unless – unless she's a ghost. I don't think I want to talk to a ghost...' she added in a whisper.

'Then maybe we shouldn't do this.' Freddie folded his arms, looking suddenly older-brotherly.

The girls stared at him in surprise.

He shrugged, turning pink with embarrassment. 'It seems bad form to summon up a ghost, especially if you're going to get all upset about it, Rose. I mean, we're dragging this spirit up from somewhere, and she might be busy, and then to have you crying all over her...'

Gus snorted. 'Busy!'

'Well, what do ghosts do?' Freddie shrugged. 'I've never met one.'

Bella looked at him with her head on one side. 'Are you scared?'

Freddie started to deny it furiously, but Rose just shuddered. 'I am. I don't think I'd be scared of just any ghost – I've seen so many strange things since I came here. But this ghost actually belongs to me, and that's scary.' She gripped the edges of the mirror frame tightly, forcing herself not to put it down and walk quickly out of the room. 'I don't think it's scarier than the spiders' webs, though. So we should do it. Do we have to do anything special, if we think we might be summoning a ghost?' she asked Gus, her voice squeaking at the edges.

Gus frowned at the glass. 'I think we should be a little careful what we invite into the house. We're opening a door, in a way.' He was kneading his front paws against the tabletop, in the way he did when he was anxious.

'Practically the first time I met you,' Rose said, 'you'd opened a door in this very room, and you were fighting off a mist-monster – and don't tell me not to call it that, Freddie!'

Gus, for once, looked embarrassed. 'That was research…' he muttered. 'Freddie encouraged me. And that just means you know how dangerous it is to go around summoning things.'

Rose sniffed. She had in fact seen off the mist-monster, or elemental spirit or whatever it was called, by thumping it on the nose, which it hadn't expected. But when she and Freddie and Bella had been trapped by a crazed magician who wanted to use their blood for a spell, Freddie had summoned up the mist-monster again and it had devoured Miss Sparrow in what looked like a couple of smallish gulps. Gus was right.

They did need to be careful.

'Well, if something bad was coming, you'd smell it, wouldn't you?' she asked. 'Or it would make your whiskers go all tingly.'

'Oh, I'm not saying we shouldn't do it,' Gus told her airily. 'I just like you to be properly aware of what you're doing, that's all.'

'So that you can rescue us when we do it wrong?' Freddie raised his eyebrows.

'Indeed.' Gus gave him a slit-eyed smirk. 'Or not. Anyway, Rose, no. Just do what you were doing before.'

Rose shrugged. 'All I did was look.'

'Then look again.' Gus was starting to sound impatient. 'And look carefully. Be watchful.'

Rose shivered, but she gripped the mirror frame tightly, and felt Freddie and Bella draw closer, leaning over her shoulders to stare in too. There was a distracting aroma of buttered toast.

Rose concentrated hard on the glass, pleading with it inside her head. *Tell us what happened. I want to see. I want to know why – why she left me. But not a ghost. Please. Unless there's nothing else...*

The blackness took longer to settle into the mirror this time, perhaps because they were all weary. But at last the glass clouded, like paint settling into clear

101

water, and turned a murky black. Rose's shoulders tensed, sensing that something was approaching. The blackness seemed to be tunnelling back, heading away to some strange place. Now, the odd silvery mist that Rose had seen before was flowing towards them through the dark. As it came closer, Rose's breath caught in her throat, and she had to force herself to start breathing again. It was a figure.

Her mother's ghost.

SIX

Rose let out a muffled gasping sob, and almost dropped the mirror. Only Freddie grabbing it saved them from losing the vision entirely. As it was, the figure in the mirror seemed to recoil, cowering back into the darkness, and darting anxious glances this way and that, as though she wasn't sure she was doing the right thing.

'Rose, stop it!' Freddie snapped. 'Pull yourself together, we nearly lost it there.'

Rose gulped. How could Freddie be so cruel? 'She's dead. She is, after all. That's a ghost, isn't it? So my mother is dead. I don't think I can bear to talk to the ghost of my mother. I thought I could do it, but I can't!'

'Then you'll never know what happened. Which is worse?' Gus was standing on Freddie's shoulders, hissing in her face, and Rose wept, turning away from them, and from the silver figure in the mirror.

'I don't know, I don't know!'

'Ssshhh!' Bella poked Rose in the ribs. 'Stop squabbling, all of you, and look. I don't think that's anyone's mother, Rose. That's a little girl.'

Rose looked back around slowly. She wouldn't have put it past Bella to try to trick her into looking, so she couldn't pull away.

But Bella was right. Lingering in front of them, just inside the mirror frame, as though she didn't dare climb out into the room, was a ghost-girl. She actually looked older than Bella herself, Rose's age, or even a little more. But Bella would never admit how young she was.

'She doesn't look anything like you, or the portrait of Miranda,' Bella pointed out. 'As much as one can tell, when she's all silvery-grey. Do you think that's because she's been living in a silver mirror?' Then she nudged Rose's shoulder. 'You'd better talk to her, Rose, she's staring at you.'

She was, her eyes round with wonder, and fear, and deep confusion.

Rose swallowed. 'Who are you?' she asked quietly,

trying not to sound too accusing. She felt accusing –
she wanted to demand what this girl was doing coming
out of her mother's mirror.

The ghost blinked, her washed-out features seeming
to frown. 'Eliza. I'm Eliza. Don't you know me, Miss
Miranda?'

'Rose, she thinks you're your own mother!' Bella
hissed excitedly. 'She must have known her.'

'I'm – I'm not Miranda,' Rose stammered, and the
ghost-girl leaned closer, pressing up against the mirror
glass, frowning and peering at her.

'Miss Miranda? Maybe – maybe you're not. You
look like her, but I haven't seen her in such a long
time.' She pulled away from the glass, and rubbed her
hands over her face as though she was confused.
'I don't understand. Who are you? You're too young
to be Miss Miranda, I think. Unless… I don't
understand,' she repeated wearily.

'You're a ghost. Do you understand that?' Gus asked
suddenly, and the girl jumped, pressing her hands over
her heart.

'Mercy me!'

'Your heart isn't racing, however much you may
want it to,' Gus pointed. 'Think. You're a ghost, aren't
you?'

'Don't be cruel to her,' Rose whispered, feeling

rather shocked. It seemed that Gus was being dreadfully callous.

'She'll be no use to us until she understands what she is.' Gus didn't even turn and look back. 'What are you?'

The little figure drooped sadly and nodded. 'A ghost. A dead thing, sir.'

'Gus, this is mean!' Rose hissed.

'Do you want to know what happened to your mother, or not?' Gus snapped, his whiskers vibrating with irritation. 'Don't be so soft. The dead are dead, and if she doesn't understand where she is in time, she can't show us what happened, can she?'

'I still don't see why you have to talk to her as if she's a slave!' Rose stopped, and frowned slightly at him. 'Unless…you're afraid of her, aren't you? Is this why you kept uttering all those dire warnings about doors?'

'Shut up.' Gus's shoulder bones were sticking out of his fur, and his tail was fluffed out like a bottle brush. 'You dislike spiders, I dislike the dead. They play tricks. That's all there is to it. Now talk to this one, so we can send it away.'

'Don't send me away,' the little silvery figure pleaded. 'I'll be good. I'll tell you what you want to know. Please.'

'Who are you, please?' Rose asked, very politely, trying to counteract Gus's rude treatment of the little ghost.

'Eliza Lampton, miss,' the ghost told her promptly. She wrung her wispy hands nervously, and put her head on one side. 'If you're not Miss Miranda, miss, might you be so good as to tell me who you are? You look the very spit of her, miss, when she was a good bit younger, that is.'

Rose glanced quickly at Gus, suddenly unsure whether telling one's name to ghosts was dangerous, but he was sitting on Freddie's shoulder watching like a disapproving statue. Feeling absurdly shy, she explained, 'My name is Rose. I don't have a surname, not a proper one. I came from an orphanage, St Bridget's. But I think – I don't know for certain – I think I may be your Miss Miranda's daughter. Oh! Don't do that, please, don't go!'

The silvery girl was drawing backwards away from them, her hands over her mouth, and her eyes huge in that pale face surrounded by strange, dark, wet-looking hair. She was muttering something behind her hands, and Rose had to lean forward to catch what she was saying. It felt as if she was reaching into the dark tunnel.

'I remember! I remember!' The ghost sat down in

the darkness, and wrapped herself around her knees. 'I remember it all…' she whispered at last, looking up at them, as though she was the one who was haunted, and not them at all.

'Can you come out of the mirror?' Rose asked her suddenly. She wanted the poor little thing to come out, and sit with them. Perhaps even to hold her hand, while she told them the story.

The ghost shook her head. 'I don't think so, miss. Not yet, anyway. I've been in here a while. I'm tied.' She sat up, and stretched out her hands to either side. To Rose it looked as though she was only stretching her fingers into nothing, but clearly she could feel the darkness pressing against her. 'Besides…' she glanced nervously at Gus. Clearly she liked the look of him as little as he liked her.

'Keep her shut away in there,' Gus muttered. 'Then we're all safe. Her as well.'

Rose glared at him. 'Eliza, how did you know my mother?'

Eliza wriggled closer to them, and stared out at Rose. 'I was her maid, miss.'

Rose nodded slowly. She should have expected it, she supposed. A grand young lady like Miranda Fell would of course have a personal maid. There was a strange sort of symmetry to it, as well, that she should find her mother's maid. Her life had been far more like Eliza's than her mother's.

'I went with her, miss, when she ran away with John Garnet – him that was your father, miss.'

Rose gasped. 'Did you? No one told us that. So you know what happened? Why they left me? You know why I ended up at St Bridget's?' In her eagerness to hear, she reached out her hand to Eliza, wanting to touch the little kneeling figure, to show her how important this was. Her hand slipped into the darkness inside the mirror, and she yelped at the sudden cold.

'Come back!' Gus hissed, and he raked his claws over her wrist. Rose pulled her hand back sharply, and sucked the long scratches, glaring at him. 'What did you do that for?' she mumbled.

'Who knows where you would have ended up, stupid girl. Be careful! What did I say to you before we started this?'

'But she isn't some horrible thing we're opening a door to,' Rose argued back.

'We don't know what she is. She may have been Eliza Lampton once, who's to say she hasn't changed? Don't touch her, for all our sakes!' Gus stared suspiciously into the mirror, and the ghost stared back, looking anxious.

'Stop squabbling!' Bella leaned closer to the mirror.

'Eliza, will you tell us about Miss Miranda? How she ran away, and what happened after?' She didn't say please, and her tone was imperious, but it seemed to be what Eliza was used to. She nodded eagerly, looking almost relieved. She was used to orders.

'Yes, miss.' She closed her eyes, remembering. 'Miss Miranda asked me to help her pack. She swore me to secrecy.' There was pride in her voice. 'She told me the master would never let her and John Garnet be together, and they were going running off to London to get married. She'd had a fight with him, you see. We all heard the shouting, all us servants. Miss Miranda wanted me to fetch her a carpet bag or some such, out of the attics. She couldn't go up there without people noticing, you see.'

'She must have trusted you,' Rose murmured.

Eliza nodded proudly. 'And she never put a spell on me, miss, even though she could have done. She knew I'd not tell her secrets. So I fetched her a bag, and I fetched one for myself and all. I told her I was going with her. Well, she tried to say no, and she was that embarrassed, poor dear, because she had to tell me she'd not be able to pay my wages any longer. She knew the master would cut her off without a penny, mean old skinflint that he was. She'd be living on what John Garnet could earn for them, and he'd have no

110

references from the master, would he? So it would be a labourer's wages, if they were lucky.'

'But she was a magician! Couldn't she use her magic?' Bella sounded disgusted.

Eliza shook her head. 'She didn't know how to do much that was useful with it, miss. It didn't cook the dinner, or wash the clothes, and she couldn't do any of her grand spells, in case the spies her father had put after them found out, you see? She used to make a lovely warm fire, though, I'll say that.'

'Where did you go, when you got to London?' Freddie asked curiously.

'Some nasty low place close by Covent Garden,' Eliza sniffed. 'Miss Miranda didn't like it, but she didn't say a thing. She was good like that, and she didn't want to hurt his feelings. It was all they could afford, specially as they'd had to buy a marriage licence with his savings.'

Rose nodded thoughtfully. She could imagine her mother's life after her elopement much more easily than the pampered existence she'd had before. She had never lived in the London slums herself, but many of the other girls at St Bridget's had arrived half-grown, when their families had been wiped out by hunger, or by some terrible sickness that had spread through the city. They had hated being confined to an orphanage,

111

but they'd regarded three meals a day (even if mostly cabbage), and an outfit of clean clothes that almost fitted, as the height of luxury.

'Did he get a job?' she asked. 'My – father?'

Eliza nodded. 'As a porter, miss. Unloading the carts bringing the fruit and vegetables to the market. They were so pleased. It was a cruel, hard job, but he was used to working out in the open air, from being a gardener. And soon enough we worked out that she was having you, and she was going around in a dream-world. I'd never seen her that happy, never.'

Rose found she was smiling. 'They wanted me, then?' she whispered.

'Wanted you?' Eliza snorted. 'You'd think a baby was something that had never happened before. Your father, he made you a cradle out of fruit boxes, and the toys he carved! A Noah's ark, with all the animals, all lined up waiting. She even sewed for you, miss! And for Miss Miranda, that wasn't usual. She hated sewing. Mind you, she was cheating, I'm sure. She could never have made those little dresses without a spell to speed the sewing.'

Bella looked envious. 'I want that spell,' she whispered.

'It was almost the only magic she did while they were living there, miss, that and keeping the fire going. She was sure her father still had his spies out, she didn't want to get caught. And she never said, but I think she was sick of it, anyway. Magic reminded her of her family, you see, and the way they'd cut her off. All the magicians she knew, they all thought she was mad, she said. She didn't want anything to do with them, or their magic.'

'What about Miss Fell? Miss Hepzibah Fell, I mean?' Rose asked. 'We know her – now, in our time. She didn't cut Miranda off, did she?' Rose gripped the mirror frame tightly.

Eliza smiled. 'No. Miss Miranda said she wished she could tell her aunt where she was going, but she was right under her brother's thumb. He'd have it out of her faster than a greased rabbit, Miss Miranda reckoned, and he'd make her life a misery doing it. Miss Hepzibah was safer not knowing.'

Rose drew in a shaky breath of relief. She hadn't known how important it was for that to be true. Even though Miss Fell had been lying to her, or at least not telling her the truth, for ages, she desperately wanted to be able to trust her. But it made her grandfather sound fearsome, if he was someone who could terrorise Miss Fell.

Bella was frowning thoughtfully. 'I wonder if it was Miranda leaving that made Miss Fell so…well, you know. Stiff-spined. She said she fought with your grandfather, and left because she was so angry. That doesn't sound like the same person Eliza's talking about. I can't imagine Miss Fell under anyone's thumb now, can you?'

Rose let out a nervous giggle at the thought, but then she nodded. 'I think my mother did her a favour.'

'What went wrong?' Gus leaned in closer to the mirror from Freddie's shoulder. His ears were laid back, and he looked and sounded fierce.

Eliza darted back as though he'd aimed a blow at her, and Rose wondered if he had, by magic. She gave him a stern glare, and he gazed coldly back. Rose shuffled her feet, embarrassed. Sometimes she forgot that Gus was probably a great deal older than she was, and certainly a great deal better at magic.

'Wrong?' Eliza quavered. 'Oh! He died, sir.'

'Oh!' Rose whispered. 'John Garnet? My father died?' For a few moments it had been such a lovely story, she had almost seen it, a little room, warm with firelight. The cradle ready, and the line of little wooden animals watching over it. Hints of it, little glints, had moved in the mirror behind Eliza, she was sure. Now there was only darkness again.

Eliza nodded. 'It was a horse, miss. One of the carthorses, with a load of cabbages. Trampled, he was.

114

It was awful. I thought Miss Miranda would die herself, she was that stricken. He'd made a little mouse for the ark, the night before, the size of a fingernail, it was. She sat there holding it, and crying because there was only one.'

'She'd left everything to marry him, and he was gone, just like that,' Rose murmured. 'I would be too. Cabbages!' she added, with a choking gasp of horrified laughter. 'I'm surprised it wasn't fish,' she sobbed.

'Oh, there, miss...' Eliza wrung her silvery hands, and then stretched out towards the glass nervously, dabbing at it with her fingers, as if she wanted to reach through and touch Rose. 'It's only vegetables, at Covent Garden. Oh, I can't, I can't... You!' she hissed at Bella. 'Put your arms around her! Miss, I mean,' she added hastily.

Bella did as she was told, patting Rose a little awkwardly, and even Gus stepped from Freddie's shoulder to hers, and nudged her cheek. Freddie took a step backwards and offered Rose his handkerchief from a safe distance.

'So what did she do?' Rose whispered sniffily at last. 'She can't have gone back. Did she die too?'

Eliza shuffled regretfully, winding her fingers into the strings of her apron. Clearly she didn't want to say.

'Tell me!' Rose snapped, and felt guilty when the

115

little ghost's eyes went round and fearful, though not as guilty as she'd thought she would.

'She used her magic, miss. She had to, you were well on the way, so she couldn't do anything heavy, like. She didn't want to – she thought her father would find out, and come after her. But she didn't have a choice. She sent me to put a little card up in the window of the Three Bells, the pub down the street. *Any Tasks Undertaken*, it said. *Discretion our watchword. No love philtres.* Miss Miranda said those would probably make our fortune, but she couldn't bear it.'

'Did he find you then? Mr Fell?' Freddie asked. He was so fascinated he'd forgotten to avoid tearful girls, and had crept up close to the mirror again.

Eliza shivered. 'No.'

Freddie drew in an excited, anxious breath. 'But someone did?' he guessed, leaning close to hear Eliza whisper.

'It were all right at first,' the little servant muttered. 'She did little things. Found a lady's lost lapdog. Found an old man's will for his son, when he'd died and not said where he'd hidden it. But then she started to get known, you see? She was getting a reputation. And this shifty-eyed man came. He wanted her to look at some gold coins, and see if they were real, or forgeries. He said someone had used them to pay him.' She shivered again. 'And if they did, I feel sorry for them, I truly do.'

'The coins were fake?' Gus asked, with a professional sort of interest. Mr Fountain had made his fortune as the country's only successful alchemist. Gus, as his familiar, clearly regarded this as research. He had stopped being quite so unpleasant.

Eliza nodded. 'Very clever fakes, Miss Miranda said. With a spell on them to make them even better.'

'Hmf.' Gus considered this, his eyes hooded.

'When Miss Miranda told the man, I could see he weren't happy,' Eliza whispered, her eyes dark with the memory of fear. 'I couldn't tell if what he'd said was the truth, or whether he'd made those coins himself, and he just wanted to see if she could tell.'

'You think he was the counterfeiter?' Gus demanded sharply, and Eliza nodded very slightly.

'I thought so. Miss Miranda was just glad he paid her in the real kind. She was past caring, poor thing.' Eliza eyed Rose almost accusingly. 'Made her life a proper misery those last few months, you did.'

Rose nodded mutely, unsure if she should apologise. It was the strangest conversation.

'It was the very next day that *he* came.' Now Eliza was visibly trembling. It made her strange silvery skin shimmer all over, and she wrapped her arms around her chest, as though to try and hold herself still.

Rose found herself trembling too. 'He?' she whispered.

'The counterfeiter told him. He must've done. Miss Miranda was on his patch, see? He came, and he had the card from the Three Bells' window. He said we didn't need it any longer, and somehow, when he said it, I knew it was true. He had the gift. He could make you believe anything, Pike could.'

'Pike? That was his name?' Bella sounded contemptuous, but Eliza frowned at her.

'One of the stableboys told me once what a pike is – I'd never known before. Great big river fish, all greyish green and spotted. They lie in wait for the smaller fish, hanging still in the water, hardly even twitching their fins. And then a poor little fish swims past, and the pike leaps on it, and swallows it whole with its huge great teeth. They're so crazed, sometimes they try to eat a fish that's as big as they are, and die trying. Nasty, evil things.'

'They taste nice, though.' Gus's bright pink tongue stuck out of his mouth for just a second, and his eyes misted with the memory.

'Stop it, Gus. He likes fish,' Rose said apologetically. 'Did he bewitch Miranda too?'

Eliza shook her head thoughtfully. 'Not at first. It took him a lot longer to catch her. She was sitting

118

there, watching him drink tea, and she had a look on her face – same sort of look as that one had just now –' she pointed to Bella – 'like she thought he was common. And when he started saying that she was on his territory, she just laughed. But she was so tired, what with the baby, and grieving for Mr John. He went on, and on, and on at her. She didn't see what he was doing. She was such an innocent, you see. All the time he was wrapping her in layers and layers of magic. Like a spider wrapping up a fly. The more he talked, the weaker she got, like he was drawing the strength out of her, sucking out her insides.'

'Ugh.' Bella shuddered.

Eliza nodded, and leaned closer to the glass again. 'And when she was all drained out, he sent *his* magic into her. She was like a puppet, dancing on strings.' She sighed. 'I couldn't tell her. I could see it, but he wouldn't let me tell her. I couldn't move, let alone speak. I just sat there in the corner, and she thought I was being a good, quiet servant, and all the time I was raging and screaming inside!'

'What did he do to her?' Rose begged, her nails digging into her palms, sure that she was about to hear how her mother had died.

Eliza laughed sadly. 'He told her to pack. She only had her little carpet bag, and another bundle of the

119

baby clothes. He had her walking out of the door, and I was still sitting there on the stool in the corner. But then she stopped – she didn't see me – but she knew something was wrong. She knew I was missing. Even though he had her all wrapped up in a spell, she remembered me.' The pride in the little ghost's voice was pitiful. 'She made him stop, and bring me too.'

Gus twitched his whiskers. 'You *wanted* to go? To be kidnapped by this powerful underworld magician?'

Eliza simply stared at him. 'Where else would I go? Miss Miranda knew I didn't have anywhere else. I couldn't have gone home, even if I could find the fare for the stage from somewhere. And it would have to have been somewhere a decent girl wouldn't even think of, mind you. No, if I'd have gone home, my dad would have sent me right away again. My family lived in a tied cottage, one that belonged to Mr Fell. If they'd taken me back after the way I'd run off with Miss Miranda, my whole family would have been out. We'd all have been in the poorhouse. I burned my boats when I went with her, Mr Cat.'

Gus laid his ears back a little at that, but he didn't complain. Rose could see that much as he disliked ghosts, he was developing a grudging respect for this one and her loyalty.

'That's how Miss Miranda Fell and me, we joined

the Pike gang.' Eliza giggled, but she didn't sound as though she really thought it was funny. 'The most bloodthirsty gang of murdering thieves you're ever likely to meet.'

'She didn't – she didn't work for them?' Rose asked, her voice horrified.

Eliza sighed irritably, a puff of chilly, silvery not-breath smudging the mirror glass. 'Of course she did! She hadn't a choice! Do you not understand anything? They made her do it. I cleaned and cooked and ran errands, and did what I was told, and Miss Miranda did the same. She did what she was told.' Her shoulders drooped. 'If it makes you feel any better, miss, I don't think she ever actually killed anybody.'

Rose gasped. 'You don't *think*?' She shivered, and her fingers seemed to grow cold and dead. And she dropped the mirror.

SEVEN

'Catch it!' Bella squealed, and Rose stared at her hands in dismay. She had no feeling in her fingers – it was as if they didn't belong to her any more. The mirror seemed to spin as it headed for the floor, and a thin, despairing wail floated up.

'Oh, no, no…' Rose moaned, as it hit the floor with a thud.

Bella snatched the mirror up. 'Eliza's not there, but it isn't broken!' she cried thankfully. 'Oh, Miss Fell would have killed us. Rose, what were you doing?'

'My mother was working for a bad magician! For a gang of murderers! That's probably how I ended up in the orphanage, Bella, someone fought back and killed her. She was a criminal!' Rose stared down at her fingers. They felt just like they usually did, and she clenched them, digging her nails into her palms. She could feel that. She dug in harder, watching red half-moons flower on her skin. It hurt, which was good, because she felt as though things had changed so much in the last two minutes that it might not have done.

Through all her time at St Bridget's, she had assumed her parents were simply too poor to keep her. She had never, somehow, thought that they might be anything but honest. 'My fingers stopped working before. When Eliza said…'

'She did say she didn't think your mother had killed anyone,' Freddie reminded her helpfully.

Rose glared at him. 'Oh, wonderful! Not quite a murderer's daughter, then!'

Freddie sighed. 'She didn't have a choice, Rose. You heard what Eliza said – she was bound into a spell. It sounded like a very clever one, too. She wasn't used to dealing with other magicians, was she? Not if she'd lived most of her life in the wilds of Derbyshire, with what sounds to me like a mad family. He got her good and proper.'

Rose nodded. She set the mirror down in front of her, and gazed at it, her chin on her hands. She hoped it hadn't hurt Eliza, being dropped. 'It's what

Mr Fountain said would happen to me,' she told them, very quietly.

Freddie blinked. 'What?'

Gus was eyeing her sympathetically. 'You see now that he was right, don't you?' he asked gently.

'What did Papa say?' Bella sounded indignant. She disliked it when other people knew more about her father than she did.

'When everyone in the kitchens hated me, I was going to run away. Ssh!' She held up a hand as Freddie and Bella both started to talk at once. 'I never even tried. Your father stopped me, Bella. Him and Gus. I was going to try to make a living for myself the same way my mother tried to, finding things. Helping people. It seemed such a good idea!' She laughed hollowly. 'Gus said someone would cut me up and throw me in the river in a whole set of sacks. Or that I'd be made to work for someone awful. Like Miranda was.'

'I can't believe you were going to run away!' Bella burst out. 'You never told me!'

'You hardly ever talked to me then, except to complain that your dresses weren't properly ironed,' Rose pointed out. 'Nobody talked to me, that was the point. Even Freddie was being sniffy because he didn't want to share being an apprentice.'

'I'm sure I was not.' Freddie scowled. 'Or only a little, Rose, anyway.'

'I hated it here. I can't believe the same thing almost happened twice.' She smiled sadly. 'Perhaps I am like her.'

'But *you* have people to watch out for you.' Gus tickled her cheek with his whiskers. 'We would not let that happen to you, Rose. We didn't. Like we said then, we're responsible for you. Even though we know who your parents are now, you are still Aloysius's apprentice, and we will always be bound together. We would not let a back-street magician steal one of our children away.' He sniffed disgustedly. 'Think yourself lucky, Rose. Those Fells. Obsessed with birth and history and lineage, but not with people. They should not have let your mother out of their hands. Although...' his whiskers shimmered thoughtfully, 'it's highly possible that the girl had more fun in the year she had living in the London slums than she ever did walled up in a draughty mansion in Derbyshire.'

Rose giggled in spite of herself. 'I wouldn't let Miss Fell hear you say things like that. She'd have you turned into fur gloves.'

Gus gave her a sharp look, before obviously deciding that this counted as nervous exhaustion and not insolence to cats. 'Miss Fell might even admit the same.

She said it herself – she could not leave the Fell house until she was so angry she made a clean break from the family. I suspect she is infinitely happier for it.' He thumped Rose's arm with his lead weight of a tail. 'Now. Find that girl ghost again. I want to know what happened next, even if you don't.'

Rose nodded and picked up the mirror, a little gingerly, in case the strange thing happened to her fingers again. 'I do want to know, I suppose... Oh, of course I want to. I want to know every last bit, but I'm not sure I want to actually hear how she died. I just want to *know*.' She looked round and saw that Bella and Freddie were frowning, and Gus was giving her the look of an impatient cat, his tail slightly twitching.

'Just look into the mirror, Rose dear,' he purred, unsheathing his claws very slightly.

Rose sighed. 'Sorry.' She stared into the dark glass, searching for Eliza, but only her own face stared back. The silvery ghost girl had gone entirely. 'She isn't coming back.' Her voice had risen slightly in panic.

Bella peered at the glass. 'Just do what you did last time.'

'I did!' Rose snapped. 'Nothing's happening.'

'Maybe you scared her away, dropping it like that,' Freddie said, tapping thoughtfully at the glass with one finger.

Rose shook her head. 'I can't have done. I didn't drop it that hard, did I?' she asked them pleadingly.

Bella shrugged. 'It looks like you must have done.'

Freddie nodded. 'It might have felt to Eliza like you did it on purpose,' he pointed out.

Rose stared into the mirror again, straining her eyes and her mind, but the glass remained obstinately glass. What if Eliza never came back? 'No…' she whispered. 'Please, Eliza, I need to talk to you. I have to know how it ended!'

Gus looked down at the glass, and hissed thoughtfully. 'Perhaps it didn't…'

Rose dragged her eyes away from the mirror-glass, and frowned wearily at him. 'What do you mean?'

Gus went on staring at the mirror, his tail flicking faster now. But he seemed to be angry with himself, for once. 'We could have been wrong. I've heard of the Pike gang. Notorious lot. Very savage. Mixed up in the opium trade too, I think…' He closed his eyes in a slow blink, and then looked up at Rose. 'They're still there. So why shouldn't she be?'

Rose felt the chair suddenly swing beneath her – as though a rug had been pulled out from underneath it.

'Rose!' Bella caught her hands, and rubbed them. 'She's like ice. Rose, wake up!'

Rose shook herself. Gus's words had seemed to send

her into a dream – that confused state where nothing is ever certain. The strangest things happen, but no one cares. She swallowed tightly, and whispered, 'But you said…you all said it. That I was being silly, wishing she were still alive.'

Gus wrapped his tail firmly around his paws, and stared off sideways into the shadowy corners of the room. Clearly he hated having to contradict himself. 'All I'm saying is, it may not be as much of a certainty as we thought,' he growled. 'So look in the mirror, girl.'

Rose snatched it up. Perhaps Eliza had just been shocked when the mirror fell. Surely now they would see her, edging towards them through the mist…

But there was nothing in the glass, not even the slightest silvery shimmer. Rose sat back, staring down at her hands. How could she have been so stupid and dropped the mirror? 'What am I going to do?' she whispered, more to herself than to the others.

'Miss Fell might be able to help,' Freddie suggested reluctantly. 'She must have known Eliza, if she was your mother's maid while she lived at Fell Hall. Maybe she could summon her for us.'

Bella sniffed. 'I wouldn't come, if I were a ghost and she summoned me.'

Freddie shuddered. 'Knowing her you wouldn't have a choice.'

But Rose shook her head. 'I don't think that would be a good idea. You saw how much it upset her talking about my mother. What if we tell her all this, and raise her hopes, and then we can't find her?' She swallowed. 'Or worse. If the gang did kill her, and Miss Fell has to find that out. It would almost be worse for Miss Fell than it would be for me. I've never even met her. Well, not since I was a baby.'

'Shouldn't you be calling Miss Fell Great-Aunt Hepzibah?' Freddie pointed out, with a sweet smile, but Rose shuddered.

'No. It would feel too…familiar.'

'She *is* your family!' Freddie teased, but Bella interrupted him.

'We should tell Papa instead.'

Gus nodded. 'Indeed. The sooner the better. He may even know more about the Pike gang. He has several times consulted for the police, after all.' He jumped off the table, and looked back up at Rose. 'And bring the mirror. He may also be able to compel that girl to come back and speak to us.' He was heading for the door, his tail waving grandly, so he didn't see Rose clutch the mirror tightly to her.

Rose didn't want Eliza compelled! She would tell Mr Fountain so, she resolved. It was her mirror now, after all, and her mother they were trying to find.

He wouldn't make her force Eliza out, surely?

But when they trooped down the main stairs – something which still made Rose's stomach lurch, as she had only been allowed on those stairs to clean them when she was a servant – they saw Mr Fountain fighting his way into his smart caped overcoat. The front door was open, and Rose could just see Bill haring off across the square, presumably to fetch the master a hansom cab.

'Is everything all right, sir?' Freddie asked.

'Another dratted summons to the palace!' Mr Fountain snapped irritably. Officially his post was that of a magical adviser to the Treasury – which meant that he made gold – but as he was the only magician the king trusted, he tended to be called in for everything. 'I'm going to have to start getting things wrong – being indispensible is remarkably boring. The Talish really are mounting another invasion, apparently. They've been building more ships in secret. Oh, and that's military intelligence, so don't tell anyone.'

A battered black horse cab drew up outside the house, with Bill hanging grimly on behind. Mr Fountain eyed it despairingly, and Bill shrugged and rolled his eyes as he ran up the steps.

'You said to be quick, sir!' he protested. 'Matter of life and death, you said. It goes, don't it?'

'Does it?' Mr Fountain muttered. 'I wouldn't count on it. Behave, all of you. I may not be back for dinner.' He sighed. 'Or breakfast.'

He climbed into the cab, which wobbled worryingly when he slammed the door, and bowled away, leaving the children staring at each other in the hall.

'Well, that scuppers that then,' Freddie muttered. 'Are you sure you don't want to talk to Miss Fell about it, Rose?'

'I don't think giving the house guest a heart attack counts as behaving,' Rose pointed out.

'What did you want him for?' Bill asked, keeping an eye on the green baize door to the servants' quarters, in case anyone popped out to tell him off for fraternising with the upstairs children.

'Oh! He might know!' Bella exclaimed, pointing at Bill in what Miss Fell would have called a most unmannerly fashion.

Freddie nodded. 'Of course! He knows everything that happens in the square. He talks to all the other boys, the lads from the stables, the delivery boys. Don't you?'

'That's only round here. Just because we came from an orphanage, it doesn't mean we rub shoulders with thieves' gangs!' Rose pointed out. 'I didn't know anything about the Pike gang, did I?'

'Here, don't you go getting mixed up with them!' Bill snapped, his eyes widening worriedly.

Bella smiled smugly at Rose. 'I told you. He does know who they are.'

'Do you really?' Rose asked. 'You're supposed to be respectable!'

Bill shrugged. 'Only gossip from the stables, and some of my mates from St Bartholomew's.'

'Do you know where we could find them?' Rose begged, grabbing his arm excitedly.

'No, I do not, and if I did I wouldn't tell you lot! Are you asking to get chopped up into sausage-meat patties?'

'Ugh, they don't, do they?' Bella asked, with horrified fascination.

Bill folded his arms grandly. 'So they say. Hey, Rose, what's the matter? What's she gone that colour for?'

'Her mother. She was a magician, kidnapped and forced to work for the Pike gang,' Freddie explained, putting a hand in the small of Rose's back to hold her up. 'Rose is…upset. It may have been her mother, um, mixing the sausage-meat.'

Gus, who was in Rose's arms, patted a fat paw firmly against her cheek. 'Don't faint! You'll drop me. If you really want to find her, you have to accept that you might not like what you find. Though, really, Frederick, a little tact!'

'Your *mother*?' Bill whispered, staring at Rose.

She nodded. 'And it may be that she's still alive… Miss Fell thought she was – oh. I forgot, you don't know. Miss Fell is my great-aunt.'

'That old tabby upstairs?' Bill gaped at her.

'Yes. Miss Fell thinks she would have known if my mother was dead. They were very close. So she might still be there, Bill, with this Pike gang. I have to find out, don't you see?'

Bill nodded slowly. 'But I still don't know where they hide out, Rose. And I'm not really sure I want to go asking either.' He shivered. 'That Pike – by all accounts he's some sort of monster.'

'Eliza said he was a very strong magician,' Rose agreed. 'He bound my mother in a spell to make her work for him.'

Bill looked lost. 'Who's Eliza?'

'Oh, bring him upstairs and explain it all to him!' Gus snapped. 'It's beneath my dignity to hang around in hallways. If he's missed, you can tell them Bella wanted her bedroom furniture moved, and then she didn't like it and he had to move it back again.' He leaped from Rose's arms to land with a graceful thump halfway up the stairs. 'Come along.'

*

Even once Bill understood everything that had been going on, he still maintained he couldn't tell them how to find the Pikes' hideout, however much they begged. He agreed to make very, very discreet enquiries amongst old friends from the orphanage, but that was all.

'I don't want my ears cut off, Rose,' he pointed out, as he left the workroom.

Rose sighed. 'I don't know who else to ask.'

Gus was sitting on the table, washing his ears thoroughly. 'So defeatist,' he murmured dismissively.

'So how would you do it, clever-paws?' Freddie demanded, and Gus wrapped his tail around his paws and glared at him, narrow-eyed.

'All right, all right, I apologise,' Freddie said hurriedly. 'But really, I don't see how we can find out any more about the gang.'

'Bribe the cats,' Gus told them all smugly. 'Even a common alleycat knows exactly what's happening in his territory.'

'How?' Rose frowned.

Gus shook his head, sweeping his wonderful whiskers to and fro. 'Really, Rose dear. What do cats do all day?'

'Sleep!' Freddie snorted.

'Exactly. But usually with at least one eye open, and

in a place where we have a panoramic view of our territory, and everyone who comes in or out of it. Why the governments of every independent state in the known world have not instituted a Feline Intelligence Bureau, I do not know. Paid in fish – kippers, perhaps, and smoked salmon for the lieutenant grade. Simple.'

'FIB,' Freddie snorted. 'And that's what it would be. All cats lie, Gus. They're known for it.'

Gus's whiskers gave an irritable twitch. 'Only because we're so bored.'

'Don't they need to be magical cats? How would they tell us things?' Rose frowned.

'Any cat could pass on messages. With its eyes closed and all its whiskers stuck together with fish-glue. Is it our fault if you don't understand?' He sighed. 'I will translate. But I will require lobster for this, Rose, you understand?'

Gus slipped out of the house to speak to his associates, as he called them. Rose hadn't realised that he spent time with the other cats in the square, but he assured her as he perched on the windowsill that there were several, and some of them were quite aristocratic. 'Lady Ponsonby in the corner house has a Siamese. Strange creature. I showed you him once, do you remember, when we were discussing glamours?'

Rose laughed. 'Oh, yes! The creamy coloured cat with black paws. The thin one.'

Gus glared at her frostily. 'Who is doing whom a favour, Rose?'

'Too thin,' Rose added hurriedly. '*You* are a – a majestic size.'

'Hmmm.' Gus leaped lightly down to the sill of the floor below – very lightly, considering that he really was rather a plump cat.

He was back a few hours later, yawning, and demanding sardines, which Rose had to filch from the kitchens for him.

'So what happens now?' she asked him eagerly, watching him lick the pattern off the plate.

Gus gave the plate one last careful sweep, and stretched out his front paws luxuriously, before starting to wash. 'We wait,' he told her in between swipes around his ears. 'Think, Rose. All I have done is ask them to look.'

'But how long will it take?' Rose half-wailed.

'I have no idea,' Gus said, stretching out one hind leg in a way that suggested the conversation was closed.

Rose glared at him, and considered slamming the door, but her new room was so full of lovely precious things that she couldn't bear to, in case she broke something. She had already broken the magic of her mother's mirror, she thought sadly. Her new room had a dressing table, with a pretty mirror of its own, but she had laid the silver mirror there, too. She sat on the delicately carved chair, and stroked the silver frame, rubbing it between her fingers. *Like Aladdin trying to call the genie from the lamp*, she thought, remembering the battered little book of fairy tales from the orphanage. But there was no puff of smoke, and Eliza didn't appear.

'Oh, there you are. We've got a lesson with your great-aunt, had you forgotten?' Bella caught her hand, and towed her along the passage to Miss Fell's room.

'I wish you wouldn't call her that,' Rose muttered as Bella knocked on the door. She tucked the mirror into the large pocket of her pinafore. If Eliza came back, she didn't want her to find herself abandoned.

'She is. You have to get used to it.' Bella turned the door-handle as they heard the faint voice inside telling them to enter.

Miss Fell was staring out of the window as they went in, and she beckoned them over with a thin hand.

'Look at that.'

Bella and Rose stood by the window, peering out, and trying to see what the old lady was watching. The only movement in the square was a few houses away.

A boy in uniform, just getting onto his horse, and waving to a group of girls who were crowding on the front steps of the house.

'What? Alfred Madely?' Bella asked. 'He's a twit, and his sisters are worse. But he did rescue my kite from a tree in the garden once.' She frowned. 'I didn't know he had joined the army.'

Miss Fell nodded. 'A Guards regiment, see the smart red uniform? Poor child.'

'He's at least seventeen,' Bella pointed out. 'Not really a child, ma'am.'

'He'll be lucky if he sees his eighteenth birthday,' Miss Fell sighed. 'So many years lost. All those stolen centuries.'

'But…we're winning the war, aren't we?' Rose asked. 'Mrs Jones's newspaper is always saying we've had a successful battle. We sank two Talish ships. That was in the paper yesterday.'

'They are driving us back to the coast, Rose. Soon the battles will be here instead.'

Bella nodded. 'Papa was called to the palace, Miss Fell. The Talish are planning another invasion. But… it won't really happen, will it? The Navy will fight them off. They won't ever be able to land, surely.'

Rose shook her head firmly. She couldn't imagine London full of Talish soldiers. It was unthinkable.

Surely Miss Fell was weaving this out of panic, and memories of the huge sea battle eight years ago when the Talish had last tried to invade. This invasion threat was all just smoke and mirrors, and it would die down again, like it always had. Wouldn't it?

Miss Fell sighed. 'It won't happen if your father can help it, Isabella. But sooner or later there will have to be a decisive action. A battle that turns the tide of the war for once and for all.' She watched Alfred Madely trotting out of the square on his glossy horse, his spurs jingling. 'I hope it comes soon. Before your father and the others are worn out, and all those eager children are dead.'

Rose shivered. She felt almost guilty. The country was at war, and everywhere in the streets there was a strange mixed feeling of excitement and fear. Alfred Madely's sisters had been full of laughter and kisses as they waved him off, but as he turned the corner they had clung to each other, crying.

Rose couldn't worry about it, not the way she should. Too much of her mind was taken up with thoughts of her mother.

'I don't believe it,' Freddie muttered. 'Everyone knows cats would lie as soon as look at you. This Ginger probably made it all up.'

Gus stalked majestically along the table and stared down at Freddie. He was a master at glamours, and Rose suspected he might have employed a subtle one as he walked – he wasn't normally that big, was he? He looked like a small white bear.

'Not you!' Freddie stammered.

'I will vouch personally for the honesty of my associates,' Gus hissed. 'Would you like to discuss this further?'

'No! Thank you!' Freddie quailed.

'Quite,' Gus replied witheringly. 'Now would you like to know what Ginger found out? After only a day, might I add.'

They were sitting in the workroom, where Gus had summoned them, his whiskers glittering with smug pride. Rose nodded – because she was too scared and excited to get any words out.

'Pike and his gang use a warehouse down by the river as their base. Ginger knew exactly who we meant, they've been there for years. Pike, and an odd shambling fellow who seems to be his right-hand man. And then a couple of others. Never more than four or five of them, he thinks. The warehouse looks abandoned, but behind the crumbling front, there's a whole warren of rooms. Most of them full of stolen property, apparently.'

'Did he know about my mother?' Rose blurted out hopefully. 'Had he seen her?'

Gus frowned and shook his head. 'No. But he's never actually been inside. He spends most of his time hanging around the fishermen. He's never had that much interest in Pike and his gang – no food involved, you see.' His whiskers quivered irritably. 'This is the problem with alleycats, everything has to be about the next meal. No sense of adventure, no nose for information unless it's leading to fish.'

Freddie gave a little snort that sounded like, 'Lobster?' and Gus glared at him again. 'Very amusing. I like fish, yes. But food is not my be-all and end-all. Don't despair, Rose. Your mother could still be there, tucked away inside. She's a valuable thing, remember.'

Rose managed to smile gratefully at him, but inside her stomach was jumping. What did this mean now? What were they going to do?

'Can we go and look?' she asked quietly.

Gus shook his head regretfully. 'We would be too conspicuous.'

'Oh, for heaven's sake! We're all magicians!' Freddie shouted. 'Can't we use that hiding spell the master taught us in Venice?'

Gus twitched his tail crossly. 'None of you are up to maintaining that spell for long enough.'

'Gus, we know that spell backwards!' Bella protested. 'Of course we can. Especially the three of us together, and with you there. Although, Rose, I think we should take Bill with us.'

'I could protect you,' Freddie said jealously.

'You can do spells,' Bella agreed. 'But when it comes to simply thumping someone, I'm afraid Bill is better at it than you are.'

Freddie scowled, which only made him look like an enraged white mouse, and rather supported Bella's point.

Gus gave a doubtful little sniff. 'Show me the spell,' he commanded, sitting up straight on the table and staring at them critically.

Glancing at each other, Rose, Freddie and Bella caught hands, and closed their eyes. Bella, in the middle, simply added to the power as the other two waved their free hands in a complicated gesture, at the same time picturing the images Mr Fountain had taught them. Misty silence, deep water, veils of protection. Around them a strange bubble of air suddenly appeared – visible to those outside it only as a slight shimmer, something that tugged at the corner of the eye, to be dismissed as just a shadow, or the flight of a small bird.

Inside the disguise spell, Rose opened her eyes. She

could see the room as usual, although the colours were dimmed slightly. Inside, she and Bella and Freddie seemed to have turned a strange pale silvery colour. Rose half-laughed, realising that actually they looked very like Eliza had. She could feel the weight of the mirror, dragging down her pocket. Even though there was no sign of Eliza whenever she looked, she couldn't bear to leave it in her room.

Outside, she could see Gus prowling around their spell, testing it with his whiskers, and an occasional flick of his tail.

'Mm. Acceptable. But how long can you keep it up for, hmmm?' He slid inside the bubble with them, and leaped suddenly onto Freddie's shoulder. The bubble of the spell distinctly wobbled. 'And can you keep it up when you are distracted, hmmm?' He climbed very carefully onto the top of Freddie's head, and hung down over his face, peering into Freddie's eyes upside down.

'Ow! That's my scalp you're digging your claws into!' Freddie hissed. 'And don't tickle me with your whiskers! Agh!'

'It's a test, Freddie, concentrate!' Rose murmured anxiously, pouring more of her own strength into the spell to make up for Freddie being distracted. 'Gus, that isn't fair, no one else is going to climb on his head and dangle their whiskers in his face.'

143

'They might do several worse things,' Gus pointed out. 'Such as gutting you with a dirty fish-knife.'

'No, they won't, because they won't see us in the first place. The spell works, doesn't it?' Bella said sweetly. 'Even with you attempting to scalp Freddie?'

'Hmf.' Gus released his claws, and slid gracefully back down to Freddie's shoulder. 'I suppose. And I will be there too. Very well. I will take you.'

The spell bubble flew apart as Rose let go of Bella and hugged Gus delightedly. She only stopped when she realised that Freddie and Bella were giving her a horrified look, and that she could feel Gus's tail twitching – the twitch seemed to echo all through him. 'I'm sorry,' she said hastily, putting him down very gently on the table.

Gus gave her a regal nod. 'I should think so. You must think before you act, Rose. Particularly when we are going investigating gangs of murderous thieves.'

But his fur wasn't standing on end in the slightest, and Rose couldn't help suspecting he had rather liked it.

'So. Send for that boy, and let us go.' Gus's tail gave a demanding little flick, as though he expected Bill to appear from thin air.

'Now?' Rose gasped.

Gus stared at her. 'Of course now! Why wait? It's the

middle of the morning. Not dark for hours. What are we waiting for?'

'I – I don't know,' Rose admitted. 'I just hadn't thought…*now*…'

'Rose, are you changing your mind?' Gus asked her wearily. The word *again* was strongly hinted in his voice.

'No! No, I just wasn't quite ready. But I am now.' Rose nodded firmly, and slid her hand around the cool weight of the mirror in her pocket. She would make herself ready. She had to.

'Down here? Really?' Bella asked distastefully, and Gus glared at her from Rose's arms. They were already inside the spell – before they had cast it, he had hidden in her scarf, as he was rather startling to passers-by.

'Yes, really. What, you'd like your criminals to live on a better class of street?' he asked.

'It's just so dirty,' Bella complained, lifting up one delicate foot, and inspecting her boot anxiously.

'Probably means we're getting close then,' Bill muttered. 'Still can't believe you talked me into this, Rosie. Following a cat to the Pike hideout? I must have let that house get to my head.'

They hadn't walked far. It seemed as if they had only gone a few streets beyond the shops where Rose was used to running errands for Mrs Jones.

'Are we really so close?' she asked, looking around. Gus nodded, and she felt the truth settle like a heavy weight inside her. How could she have lived this close to her mother's prison for so long, and not known? St Bridget's, the orphanage, was even closer – only a few minutes' walk, she guessed.

'Someone's coming!' Freddie said sharply.

'Shh, don't panic, they can't see us.' Gus peered ahead. 'I can't see anyone. Where?'

'There!' Freddie hissed. 'And whoever it is *can* see us. They're making straight for the spell!'

'Drat it, it must be one of the gang. I thought Eliza said only the leader was a magician.' Gus wriggled out of Rose's arms, and jumped down to the dirty stones. 'Ugh. Be ready to run.'

'No!' Rose breathed. 'It's Eliza! Look!'

The ghost-girl was hurrying towards them, looking anxious. The faint bleaching of the colours outside the spell had made it harder to see what she was from a distance, but now her silvery colour was obvious.

'Tch. I shall make a note to the master that this spell does not work on ghosts,' Gus growled.

'You came back!' Rose reached out to touch her, and then drew back again, unsure if she could. But Eliza laid a soft, transparent, silvery hand on her arm.

'You shouldn't be here, miss!'

'How did you get out of the mirror?' Freddie demanded.

Rose stroked Eliza's hand, very carefully. If she'd told herself it wasn't there, her fingers would have brushed straight through to her own sleeve. Eliza felt like a cold, silvery breath blown against her cheek.

'I thought we'd lost you,' she murmured. 'I've been carrying the mirror with me everywhere, and calling, but you never came.'

The little ghost's fingers seemed to become more solid under Rose's gloved hand. Eliza ducked her head shyly, but Rose could see that she was smiling. 'I didn't know where I was, miss. I got jolted out of the mirror somehow.'

'But how?' Freddie looked at her, frowning. 'You've been tied to it all that time. Was it because Rose dropped it?'

Eliza blinked. 'It was talking with you, sir. I think. It strengthened me.'

'Wonderful,' Gus muttered.

'When I told you, miss, about your father. I wanted to come out then, to help you. You looked so like her! But I didn't dare, quite. I'd been there so long. It got comfortable.'

'But where have you been since?'

147

Eliza shook her head, the damp locks of her hair flying. 'I dunno, miss. That house, it's full of strangeness. I got turned about, and there's things, floating…'

'Lord knows what she's interfered with!' Gus's tail lashed from side to side, and Eliza shrank back.

'I didn't touch nothing, Mr Cat. It were the same at Fell Hall. We knew not to touch, us servants. But then you went out, miss, and you took the mirror. So I tried to follow you, but it isn't easy. I'm not used to being out. I got lost, and then I felt him, too. Pike! You mustn't be round here, miss! It isn't safe, you shouldn't be here,' Eliza repeated. 'You're too close to the gang.'

'We meant to be,' Rose told her. 'We want to find my mother. If – if she's still there…' she added in a whisper. She meant, *If she's still alive.*

'You can't! You can't! It's far too dangerous!' Eliza's eyes darkened in horror.

'But if she's still there, caught by his spell, how can I leave her?' Rose caught Eliza's hands, and shivered at the strange soft ghost-touch. 'Please! You loved her too, didn't you? Don't you want to see her get away?'

'Of course! But I don't want them catching you.' She gulped, her face twisting with fright, and then hissed,

148

'Don't you see? That's how I died! I tried to stop them taking you!'

'Oh.' Rose stared at the little ghost, lost for words.

'Come on!' Eliza tugged her, her hands patting and pulling at Rose's own. Her fingers seemed to sink into Rose's skin, and Rose followed her more to stop the horrid sensation than from any strength of Eliza's.

Eliza led them further down the murky alleyway to the edge of the river. The tide was out, and a vast expanse of mud stretched out before them. The silvery ghost pattered down a set of rotting steps and out across the mud, and they followed her gingerly to an old boat, lying upside down on the mud like some strange old shell. 'Sit in here. We'll be hidden. I'll explain.'

There were several pieces of old packing case under the boat, as though this was a common haunt for someone, but even they were slimed and dirty with river water and weed, and Bella clearly couldn't stand the thought of sitting on them.

'Oh, Bella, stop it,' Rose hissed. 'Your papa will buy you a new coat if you flutter your eyelashes at him. Just sit down! I want to hear, and you do too.'

Closing her eyes in disgust, Bella did as she was told, and Eliza began to tell her story.

EIGHT

'Your mother had almost forgotten her previous life,' Eliza explained. 'She was so deep in the spell that Pike had put on her, she couldn't even remember who she was. Every so often she'd catch a glimpse – I reminded her of the way things used to be. But most of the time she thought she'd lived in the old Beloved's Import & Export warehouse for ever. That's the name of the building where Pike has his headquarters,' she explained. 'I don't know when those Beloveds last used it, but there's a big faded old sign on the waterside.'

Rose glanced back towards the building. It was a misty, grim February day, but she thought she could just see the sign Eliza meant. It was lopsided, and the wall it was hanging on didn't look much better.

'Why didn't you go to the police?' Bill asked. 'If you weren't under this spell? Didn't they let you out?'

Eliza shook her head, her eyes widening in horror. 'You don't know what they'd do! I saw them! I saw them while we was there – they cut one lad's tongue out for blabbing about a shipment, and he weren't much older than you! Besides. Miss Miranda was doing Pike's dirty work for him. I couldn't go telling, they'd have hung her too. If they ever caught them, which they wouldn't have.' She sniffed dismissively. 'Pike never got caught. That's what he had Miss Miranda for. He wrapped her up in that spell, and stole the magic out of her to make him stronger.'

Gus frowned. 'That doesn't sound right. Wouldn't her magic fight against his own, if he used it against her will? He must be a strange sort of magician.'

Eliza shrugged. Clearly she didn't know, and hardly cared. 'She was lucky she had me to look after her. She wouldn't even have remembered to eat if I hadn't made her, and she needed to, with you, miss. Not that they gave us much. Reckon they thought she lived on air, and she did, some of the time, when I couldn't wake her from the spells to have a little something.

'But then when she was near her time with you, miss, she started to break out of his magic. More and more, she was almost herself. She said you wriggled worse

151

than a squirming cat, and you kicked her, and that kept waking her up out of the magic, you see. She was worried, I could tell, about what was going to happen – how she'd look after you in that place. But at the same time, she could see that having you was going to make it harder for Pike to make her do what he wanted. Already you were breaking his hold on her. That's why she named you the way she did, when you were born.'

'What? What did she call me?' Rose was crouching on the mudflats in front of Eliza, stretching out her hands, trying to make her tell.

'Hope. That's your name, miss. Hope Garnet. You were her hope of keeping herself herself, if you see what I mean.'

Rose nodded, but then she sat back on bit of packing case. 'It didn't work, though. She didn't escape.'

Eliza shook her head, her eyes half-closing with remembered grief. 'She was worth too much to them, miss. And so were you. It was all right for the first few months. Miss Miranda – not that I should call her that, but I still can't think of her as anything else – she was careful not to let them see how much in control of her magic she was getting. She couldn't risk them finding out and Pike recasting the spell. She was working her way out gradually, like. But then he came to see her one day, and he was watching you. You'd learned to crawl, miss, and I made you a rag doll. You played with it all the time.' Eliza sniffed a laugh. 'You used to carry it around in your mouth while you were crawling. Usually, Miss Miranda would try to hide you away when he came, make sure you were sleeping, or get me to take you out to see the water, wrapped up in a shawl. He turned up unexpected that day, and she could see him eyeing you. He knew what you were. Your father might not have had magic, miss, but your mother had enough that it was bound to be bubbling over in you.' She shook her head. 'That was it. Once she saw him looking at you like that, as though you were something valuable, something he could make money out of, she knew her time was gone. She hadn't managed to drag herself out of the spell enough to escape, and she wasn't going to have you trapped there too. She didn't want you growing up as their little tame magician, never knowing right from wrong. You'd have been a monster, miss.'

Eliza nibbled on her knuckles and eyed Rose anxiously. 'That's why she did it, miss. You do see, don't you? It wasn't that she didn't want you, not at all. You were saving her, and even if you hadn't been, she adored you. That's why you had to go. She couldn't bear to see you made into one of them.' Eliza looked down at her transparent, battered boots, and then sharply up again at Rose. 'She thought you'd be better off dead.'

Rose gasped, a tiny, shocked noise that seemed to echo around the wooden ribs of the boat, and Bill put his arm around her, staring angrily at Eliza.

'You would have been!' Eliza snarled fiercely. 'You don't know what they're like, what they would have made of you!' She folded her arms, glaring at Rose. 'Don't you dare think ill of her. She couldn't do it. She said if she'd really loved you properly, she could have done. She was angry with herself for not being strong enough. I took you to the churchyard instead. So that someone would find you and take you away, look after you, and keep you away from Pike.'

'Why there? That churchyard?' Rose whispered faintly.

Eliza shrugged. 'Because it was close. I didn't have long, miss, before someone would notice I'd gone. I put you in the old fishbasket I used when they sometimes let me go to the market. Miss Miranda liked a bit of fruit, and they used to let me out to buy it for her, if Pike was feeling generous.'

Rose nodded. She had always assumed it meant her real parents had something to do with fish. 'Didn't she have anything to leave with me?' she asked wistfully. 'Even a note?'

Eliza shook her head. 'We thought about it, leaving a note. But all she could have done was use it to send you back to her family, and she thought that would be worse than useless. She said they'd fling you into an orphanage, and you'd probably be better off there anyway.'

'She should have written a note to Miss Fell,' Bella said critically.

'No, she never saw Miss Fell the way she is now,' Rose reminded her. 'When Miranda left Fell Hall, her aunt was still under my grandfather's thumb. She was the dear aunt that Miranda wouldn't tell she was running away, in case it got her into trouble.'

Eliza was nodding vigorously. 'Exactly, miss. So she decided, no note.' She was silent for a moment, wringing her hands over and over, as though she was trying to wash off some dreadful stain. 'But she did give me something for you, miss.' She looked up, her eyes pleading. 'And I'd never have taken it if I weren't so hungry. But it was silver! I knew I could get so much for it, I couldn't bear to just leave it there in the basket with you.'

'What was it?' Bella demanded. 'A ring? A necklace?'

Rose was staring at Eliza, shaking her head. 'No. Of course. It was the mirror.' She slipped a hand into the inside pocket of her coat – she had unstitched it

155

enough that she could slide the mirror in. It was the only thing she had of her mother's, and it had seemed important to bring it with them. She stroked the metal roses gently.

Eliza gave a reluctant nod. 'She said that she loved it, and she wanted you to have something that she loved. Something special. She thought maybe one day you'd get to understand the meaning of the little mouse on the back, and you'd be able to trace your family. But it wouldn't be obvious to just anyone. Only when you were old enough to know you came of a magical family, then you might be able to use it as a clue.'

She darted an anxious glance at Rose, clearly afraid of what she might say. But Rose only nodded. 'What happened?'

'I took it to a pawnshop.' Eliza wiped her ragged sleeve across her mouth, as though the thought of it still frightened her. 'I was stupid,' she added in a whisper. 'I was in a hurry. I had to get back before they missed me! So I went to a pawnshop I'd seen before, on the way to the market.'

'Too close.' Bill shook his head, and Eliza looked at him gratefully.

'Too close,' she echoed. 'They knew who I was. One of Pike's. I shouldn't have been in there with anything precious to sell. Old Mr Green, he knew he'd get on the right side of Pike if he dragged me back.' She laughed bitterly. 'Pike even let him keep the mirror, he was that grateful!'

Rose swallowed. 'What did they do?' she whispered. 'Is that how you...?'

Eliza stared at them all, her back ramrod straight with pride. 'I wouldn't tell. I'd promised Miss Miranda I'd get you away. I let her down – if only I'd done as she said and left the mirror in the basket, they'd never have known what happened to you. Miss Miranda was going to tell them you'd died of the typhus. So I wasn't having them going and finding you. I wouldn't tell.'

Rose reached out one hand, and tried to stroke Eliza's damp, rat's-tail hair. 'They drowned you, didn't they?'

Eliza smiled, an odd, proud little smile. 'Right here, miss. Pike held me under himself. It was high tide, then, of course.'

Everyone was silent for a moment, their eyes flicking nervously around the battered boat, trying not to imagine.

Bill swallowed. 'And we're going to barge into this chap's hideout?'

Rose shook her head. 'You should go back. But I have to try. If she's there, I can't leave her. Not after…' She trailed off, and waved a hand at Eliza.

No one said anything, but Bella sneaked an arm around her waist, and Gus purred. Bill and Freddie shifted closer on their boxes. They were all coming with her, she knew. Four children and a cat huddled together under the battered little boat, staring at a ghost-child.

'Then after that you haunted the mirror?' Freddie asked at last.

'It was because of the mirror I died,' Eliza explained. 'I stole it, didn't I? I think that's how it works, anyhow.'

'You've been stuck inside it all this time?' Bella shuddered.

'Not so much in it, miss…' Eliza frowned. 'Just tied to it somehow. It was like a door, but I couldn't open it. You opened it, and called me out.' She looked at Rose, her eyes thoughtful. 'What are you here for, miss?'

Rose blinked. 'To find her, of course. I have to rescue her. She'd rather have died than let me grow up there, you said so! So how can I leave her? She's my mother!'

'You have to.' Eliza shook her head firmly. 'She couldn't get away from Pike, how will you be able to do it? Besides, miss…' She hesitated. 'Pike could have done away with her, for all we know…'

'I have to know for certain,' Rose told her, through gritted teeth.

'I still don't see how you think you can get in there!' Eliza cried, sounding almost angry.

'We'll sneak in,' Freddie told her. 'We're invisible under this spell. Pike might be able to see us, but if he's the only magician, the rest of the gang won't. We sneak in and rescue her.'

Eliza stared at them doubtfully, twitching her head from side to side as she tried to see the spell. 'I can't tell no difference,' she objected.

'It's there,' Freddie assured her. 'And we can do other things too.'

'Can you show us the best way to get in?' Rose pleaded.

Eliza wrinkled her nose. 'I can try. I'm still not that good at moving about, but I can tell you what it was like back then. Might all have changed by now,' she muttered dubiously. 'Whenever there's a wrecked boat, they steal the timbers, build another little room in there. Proper rabbit warren, it is.' She shrugged, and laughed. 'Can't do me any harm, I suppose. They can't drown me again. But you're not to let yourselves get caught! They'll kill you as soon as look at you. Pike's a monster, and that other one, Jake…' She shuddered. 'He's almost worse. He smokes the opium himself, and

159

he's more like a ghost than I am. He never says nothing, and his eyes burn.' She frowned. 'Or maybe they won't kill you. If you're all magicians like Miss Miranda, they'll keep you, and that's worse.'

'I'm not,' Bill growled. 'They'll drown me.'

Freddie gave him a disgusted look. 'Run home then.'

Bill snorted. 'No chance. I'm not leaving you looking after this pair. Let's just not get caught, right?'

'I'll show you the way in I used to know,' Eliza suggested. 'Make sure your spell is working.' She crept out of the boat and stood up, brushing down her water-streaked skirts, and looking around. 'No one's moving outside,' she muttered. 'Let's go.'

They followed her, threading across the mud flats to a broken stone wall, just under the warehouse. The stones had fallen apart enough that it was relatively easy to climb up onto the wall, where there was a narrow causeway around the side of the building.

Eliza led them as they crept around the building to a window. It had been boarded up with several old bits of wood, and Eliza sniffed. 'They haven't mended it. Didn't think they would have done. Push that bit, it'll slide over. This is the way I used to take you out to see the water, miss. Come along in, but quietly.'

Bill held the piece of wood aside, and Eliza disappeared, reappearing as a beckoning hand from inside the gap. Rose and the others scrambled in, naturally lining up along the inner wall, pressing themselves back against the stones. No one wanted to go further in. They seemed to be in a store room of some kind, lined with packing cases, mostly battered and water-stained.

'Stolen cargo,' Eliza said wisely. She beckoned again from the door of the little room. 'Come on. Miss Miranda's room used to be this way. Your spell still working, is it?' She was looking at them doubtfully, as though she didn't really believe in the magic.

Rose, Bella and Freddie took hands again for a moment to boost the strength of the spell before they followed Eliza, creeping along a narrow passage. It really was built out of bits of old boat, Rose realised, as she ran her fingers over sea-worn timbers, scattered with ancient barnacles. A strange, sharp-nosed face sticking out over a doorway made them all jump, until they realised it was part of an old ship's figurehead, the paint long peeled away, leaving the face a weary grey.

'Here,' Eliza whispered. 'This is where they kept her. And you, miss.'

The doorway was low, and there was no door in it – perhaps her mother wasn't trusted enough to have a door to hide behind, Rose wondered – so they could see in as they gathered around the entrance to the room.

Eliza pressed herself against the doorframe, so close that they could see the splintered timbers through her. 'That's her...' she whispered. 'Still here!' Her whispery little voice cracked with tears, as she stared into the room. 'All this time...'

'She's there?' Rose felt strangely reluctant to look. She'd been imagining the girl from the painting, which she saw was stupid now. That girl would never have survived in here. Whoever was in that room, it wasn't the pretty child Miss Fell had loved, or even her father's stolen sweetheart, or Hope's doting mother.

But Gus was leaning forward in her arms, his whiskers twitching with interest as he peered around the tiny room.

She had to see.

'Be careful,' Freddie reminded her in a whisper. 'She's strong, remember. She might be able to see us, even through the spell.'

Rose stepped further in, brushing against Eliza, and feeling that strange faint chill again. There was very little to see. Rose's mother – if that was who it was, Rose couldn't tell – was sitting curled up on a low, narrow bed, leaning the side of her face against the wooden wall. All Rose could really tell was that her mother's hair was a little lighter than her own – and that her woollen dress was faded and worn. Rose longed to go and tap her on the shoulder, and shake her out of that sad lethargy, but she couldn't quite bring herself to do it. Not yet.

'Sshh. Someone's coming, I can hear them talking.' Eliza flitted anxiously in front of her.

Two men were walking down the passage, muttering to each other. The children whisked inside the tiny room, and then drew back against the wall, flattening themselves against the timbers. The spell would stop most people seeing or hearing them if they were careful to whisper, but they were still *there*, and fatally obvious to anyone who brushed past too close. The two men shambled up to the doorway, and paused just inside, without noticing them.

They didn't look like murderers. The most noticeable thing about them was that they both had very fine moustaches – not smartly curled ones like Mr Fountain's pride and joy, but brisk, fat ones like nailbrushes. Rose was so nervous that it made her want to giggle. The second man's hair was a dull greyish-brown, and it made him look as though he was wearing a dead mouse under his nose.

'Pike has a moustache,' Eliza whispered. 'The rest of the gang copy him.'

'Mrs Garnet, ma'am.' The man's voice was strangely nervous, which made Rose and Freddie exchange

163

a surprised glance. But then, Rose realised, it wasn't that odd. These two weren't magicians. They were like the servants at the Fountain house, forced to live with magic and not really liking it. Rose's mother was the strange, unpredictable one they had to depend on for the spells they needed. Probably the only thing they could say for her was that she was less frightening than Pike.

The figure curled on the bed shook a little, and uncoiled slowly.

Rose caught her breath, her heart suddenly beating in sickening thumps. She could feel the others, even Gus, looking at her mother, and then glancing back at her, back and forth, trying to see how similar they really were. She couldn't tell. Miranda still had a faint look of the painting in the back of the mirror, but she had changed so much. Her face was milk-pale – which was hardly surprising. Had she really been shut up in here for longer than Rose had been alive?

'You have her eyes,' Gus purred softly. 'Look. I can see you in her. We can bring her out. Somehow we will…'

Rose swallowed, and shook, and brushed her cheek gratefully against the glittering warmth of his fur.

The woman on the bed nodded at the two men wearily, and even that seemed like an effort. It was as though every move she made was fighting against the spell that bound her.

Eliza's face was scrunched up and horrified. 'He must have doubled the spell after he discovered what we done,' she breathed in Rose's ear. 'This is much worse than it used to be. She can hardly move.'

'How can she possibly do magic like that?' Rose whispered back. 'It's like she's piled down with chains.'

Eliza shook her head. 'No. That's the way he made the spell. If she's working for him, the spell lifts off her somehow. She's free – she's only free when she's working for the gang. I think Pike hoped that would break her so in the end she'd choose to join them, but it can't have worked.'

Rose nodded proudly to herself. Her mother might be working for the gang, but only because she was forced. She hadn't lapsed. But the strength of that spell was terribly daunting. How would they ever get her out of it?

The man with the dead-mouse moustache took his cap off, and stood twisting it in front of him. 'Mr Pike says, ma'am, you're to make us look like this.' He handed over a piece of paper with a rough drawing, but it was hard to see what it was from where they were squashed against the wall.

'What is it?' Rose clenched her nails into her palms.

165

'I'll look. They won't see me, miss. Only you can, because you've got the mirror.' Eliza flitted across to peer over his shoulder. 'Footmen's livery,' she whispered to Rose. 'She's changing them, so they're disguised for robbing a house.'

Rose nodded. It made sense. A tame magician must make the gang one of the most successful in London, despite their tumbledown quarters. But she still didn't understand why Pike didn't just do all this himself. Unless the gang was so huge that he was doing it too. She shivered at the thought.

Gus leaped into her arms with one of those jumps that was beyond even a cat's usual powers. 'She saw.'

'What?' Rose stared at him anxiously.

'Miranda. She saw Eliza, when she went to look at the paper. I saw her eyes move.'

'Are you sure?' Freddie muttered, next to Rose.

Gus half-closed his eyes. 'I am a cat. I am a natural predator, even without the magic. I can tell when a mouse has an itch behind its ear. Of course I'm sure, idiot boy.'

'What's she going to do?' Freddie whispered, gazing wide-eyed at Miranda. 'I thought only we could see Eliza? Can your mother see us through the spell, do you think?'

'She shouldn't be able to. We should be invisible to

166

everyone. Not ghosts, but then we'd never had one to test it on…' Gus stepped onto Rose's shoulders, standing with his front paws on one shoulder and back paws on the other. His paws felt like little rocks, pressing into her, and she could feel his heart beating against her ear. He stretched his nose out towards the three figures around the bed, his whiskers flickering around his muzzle as he searched the air. 'No. No, I don't think she can. And I don't think she can truly see Eliza either, not unless Eliza wants her to. But she knows there's something.'

Miranda raised her hands towards the two men, and Rose saw them flinch. They must be truly terrified of Pike, to let themselves be enchanted when they hated it so much.

The glamour spell seemed to stretch them – footmen had to be at least six feet tall, and preferably, if there were two in a house, they had to match. The spell changed their clothes as well, the dirty greyish fabrics flooding with blood-red, and suddenly sparkling with golden braid and polished buttons. They wore white stockings, too, which Rose privately thought was a mistake on her mother's part, as unless they had been specially bespelled to avoid mud, they would not be white by the time they got out of that horrid alleyway. But she supposed the men would just have to make do

 167

– the white stockings were what the footmen at the palace had worn, and those same buckled shoes. They must be going to rob a truly grand house, for they looked as though they would earn at least thirty pounds each a year, and who knew how much that grand livery would cost.

Freddie shot Rose an admiring glance. They knew how difficult it was to maintain one glamour, let alone two, and on such unwilling subjects. 'She's very strong,' he whispered, and Rose nodded, feeling absurdly proud.

The two men surveyed each other, looking somewhat disgusted, and then nodded their thanks to Rose's mother. Gus gave them a disparaging stare as they tramped past in the heavy buckled shoes. One of them was scratching at his powdered hair, and although they had the height of the real footmen, neither of them stood straight, as they would if they'd been trained up from boys.

The children listened to them trudging away down the passage, making rude comments about each other's outfits. Then they focused their attention, again, on the figure they had come to see. She was sitting tensely on the edge of the low bed, her hair, still pretty with its bronze-coloured streaks, trailing down past her shoulders. Perhaps they wouldn't let her have hair pins, Rose wondered. In case she did something awful with them.

As they watched, she pushed down hard against the bed with her fists, and stood up unsteadily, stretching out a foot to take a step into the centre of the room. She turned her head from side to side, her eyes wide and grey in the dim light. 'Who is there?' she asked, her voice dangerous.

Rose flinched from it. It was the voice of someone who had spent the last several years never able to rest. How could she have slept, with a gang of thieves around her? She had been on guard, all the time, and now she was fighting. One hand went up into the air, and started to pull, like someone bundling washing off a line, reeling it in.

Rose and the others felt the spell tugging away from them, pulling at their clothes and hair like a fitful wind. Bella, the youngest and least practised in her spells, twirled around, her skirt spinning, and fell straight into Rose's mother's hands, gasping in fright.

Miranda gripped her by the shoulders, a strange, half-there child, still disguised by the rags of the spell, but already starting to fight back like a little wildcat.

'Stop that!' Miranda shook her, just a little, and Bella seethed, her fingernails reaching out to scratch and tear. But she couldn't free herself from that tight grip.

169

'What *are* you? A magician's child? What are you doing here?' Suddenly she caught Bella even tighter, and pulled her forward to look closely at her face, scanning her with eyes that were doubtful and confused. As she stared at Bella, the little hint of hope in her eyes died away, and she shook her head. 'No. No, you're not. And too young, anyway... What are you doing here, child? Is this some new trick of Pike's?'

'Please let her go.' Rose pulled the spell off herself, with the same gesture her mother had used, and stepped forward. 'She isn't the one you're looking for. We came to find you. She doesn't mean you any harm, she's only frightened. Bella, *stop it*!'

'More of you!' Miranda muttered, looking around her wildly as Freddie revealed himself and Bill. But then her eyes fixed on Rose, and she seemed to turn even paler, although Rose would not have thought it possible.

'*Hope...*' she whispered.

Rose nodded. It didn't feel like her name, but somehow it seemed to catch her, and tug at her insides, so that she took another step forward, her feet faltering. 'Yes...' she murmured huskily.

Her mother let go of Bella, and reached out her arms, but before Rose could take another step towards her, her mother suddenly shrank back, her mouth twisting in pain. Her arms slammed straight to her sides, and she writhed, as though she were in agony, and screamed out loud.

'What is it? What's happening to her?' Rose cried.

'It must be the spell,' Gus said swiftly. 'She was too happy. There was an alarm set into the magic. Get away, quick. Run!' He leaped down from Rose's shoulders, and tried to herd them all out of the door, but Rose could not be torn from the sight of her mother, quivering and ashen-faced in the middle of the room, and Bella had collapsed against the bed. Bill and Freddie were trying to pull Rose away, but she struggled, and wouldn't let them.

A thundering rush of feet sounded from the passageway, and then the door was full of angry faces.

NINE

'She is my daughter. She is my daughter.'

She said it again and again and again, in a dull, mechanical voice, and it was clear from the twitching and bulging of her eyes, and the way her lips were drawn back over her teeth, that she did not want to say it all.

A tall, pale, red-haired man, whose moustache was a glorious fiery explosion, came into the room, smiling brightly. 'Is she? Is she now? This is our little stolen baby?' He stopped in front of Rose, held tightly by one of the footmen, who had been the first to come racing back when Miranda began to scream. He lifted her chin in his hand. 'I hardly need to ask. You look very like your mother, girl. So. What happened to you?

Where did you go? Hey?' His voice was not unpleasant, and he did not swear, but Rose had the most terrifying sensation of a banked-up fire. It was as though old turf had been laid across the embers to keep the fire going through till morning. Then, when someone poked it, it would spring up into a blaze again, and consume anything that came near it.

She stared back at him, too frightened to speak, and had the sense to realise that this was a good thing, and that being dumb with fright might be useful.

'She hasn't her mother's wits, then?' He turned to Miranda, and waved a hand sharply across her mouth. She broke off mid-sentence, gasping, as though someone had poured a jug of cold water over her. Her eyes stayed desperate. 'I – don't – know.' The words seemed dragged out of her.

'And the rest of them. Four.' He looked from Bella, to Freddie, to Bill. 'Three little rich brats, and a servant.'

Rose realised with a start that the servant was Bill, and not her. She supposed she shouldn't have been surprised, since she had her good clothes on. There was no mention of Gus or Eliza. Rose searched the room as carefully as she could, imprisoned against the brass buttons of a scarlet footman's coat. No, Gus was gone. And presumably Eliza could melt through walls, or something like. She couldn't be shut away. But then,

173

neither could she manipulate locks, or carry keys, with her wispy fingers. It was better to pin their hopes on Gus.

They needed someone. The more Rose saw of Pike, the stranger and more powerful he seemed, not like any other magician she had met. The magic seemed to be spilling out of him, so that his hair glittered like red-golden wire, and his eyes burned. Even his voice, soft though it was, wrapped round her and pulled, holding her like silken ropes. Was it the same spell he had used to entrap her mother? Her eyes as wide as a startled rabbit, Rose stared at him. She didn't think he was even trying.

'Ransom,' Pike muttered, fingering the braid on Bella's favourite velvet cape. 'Or are we better off keeping you?'

Bella was standing petrified, her face pale with fear – the colour even seemed to have leached out of her blonde curls, so that she looked like carved marble, something that should have been on a grave. Freddie had fought so much against the huge man who had seized him that they had tied him up, and shoved him onto the bed. Now his eyes blazed furiously over the dirty cloth they'd bound his mouth with.

Creeping from child to child, Pike sniffed fiercely, like some sort of hunting dog. It was horrible having him so close. He smelled of metal, and his eyes were a pale shade of blue, so pale it was almost white, like china. His hair looked red, but Rose could see many colours in it, like flames in a fire, as he sniffed and prowled around her. 'This one we'll definitely keep,' he muttered. 'I can smell it on her. Everywhere. Buckets of it. You should be proud of your daughter, Mrs Garnet,' he called, with a malicious little grin.

He tweaked one of Bella's curls, and stroked one finger down her stony cheek. Rose, watching, waited for Bella to bite him, but she seemed to have disappeared inside herself, and did nothing. 'A great well of it, but too far down, and at the same time oozing out of her skin. She doesn't know what she's doing with it yet. Dangerous.'

He was enjoying himself, Rose could see, sniffing out their magic, and perhaps because Freddie was bound, Pike wasn't as cautious as he should have been. He bent over close to Freddie, and then reeled back with a cry of shock, his blazing red hair truly blazing now. Freddie had always been good at fires.

It went out, of course, in seconds, but it left an ugly scorched patch all down one side of Pike's head, and Freddie was laughing, you could see it behind the gag – and even worse, some of the gang, those huge men pressed into the tiny room, were smirking a little too.

 175

Pike hissed with fury, and hurled Freddie against the wall, with a dreadful soft crunching sound. Rose cried out in horror, and even Bella woke up and gasped. Bill struggled in his captor's arms, but the man hit him carelessly, like he'd push away an over-excited dog, and Bill reeled and sagged.

Stop it! Rose shouted, but silently, inside all their heads, even somehow Bill's, who she had never known she could reach before. *Just don't. We can't fight them now, we have to wait, and – and sneak. Pike is better at fighting magic than we are, and they don't care very much if they kill us.*

She had to strain her mind to hear Freddie's reply, the faintest thread of a whisper, but at least it meant he was alive, and conscious. *Actually, they do care. I think they'd rather enjoy it.*

'That Pike is over the moon,' Bill muttered. 'Three of you! He thinks all his Christmases have come at once.' He hesitated. 'They ain't never letting us go, you know that, don't you?'

Rose didn't say what they were all feeling. That they might be shut up for ten years, just like her mother. They had been so close. It had been stupid, she supposed. They should have been more careful, watched and waited for longer. But she couldn't wait.

It wasn't fair to expect her to wait, was it? Not when her mother was only the width of a room away?

'Gus will have gone to fetch Papa.' Bella nodded as she said this, as though she was trying to convince herself. There was no getting around the fact that Gus was a cat, and his feelings and attitudes and, above all, his sense of time, could be very different from everybody else's. Despite his criticism of other cats, Gus on a life-or-death mission could still be easily distracted by a passing sardine (even if tinned).

'And there's Eliza,' Rose added. 'I think she'll come back. I think so. But she must have been terrified, seeing Pike again. And it might take her a while to find us, if she ran far. She'll have to try and find the mirror again.'

The men had bundled them down into a tiny, cramped little room, which seemed not just to have been made from a boat's timbers, but to be the tiny cabin at the bow end of a smallish fishing boat, transported in one huge piece. Surely it had been done with Pike's magic, for Rose could not see how it could have been carried. The hatch they had been shoved in by was extremely thoroughly locked, with a sort of magical seal that had burned Rose's fingers when she'd tried to push it delicately away.

Would the magical locks stop Eliza getting in to find

177

them? Rose wasn't sure. If she came back, perhaps they could send her to fetch Miss Fell, if Gus hadn't thought of that already.

Freddie had the marble light he had made in Miss Sparrow's cellar all those months ago, and they had all put extra strength into it, but it was still dim and greyish inside the boat. It still smelled of fish, too.

'How long do you think we've been here?' Bella asked irritably.

Freddie frowned. 'Only a few hours. I wonder if they're going to feed us. It ought to be teatime. Or maybe past teatime by now.' He looked wistful, and Rose could tell he was thinking of buttered crumpets. They were his favourite. She stared at him in the dusky light. She was hungry too, but she didn't want to eat. She thought she might be sick if she did. Her stomach kept twisting and jolting every time she thought about Pike, and what he might make them do. He had imprisoned her mother for more than ten years. How long would he keep them?

'For always,' Bill said dully, beside her, and Rose jumped.

'How did you know what I was thinking?'

He blinked at her owlishly. 'Didn't you say it out loud?'

178

'No. I never knew you could hear me speaking in your head.'

Bill shrugged. 'Didn't do anything. Just listened, and there you were.'

'We can't stay here for always, Bill. We'd – I don't know – wilt. We'd die in here.'

'Maybe not in here. He'll move you out of here once he's got you properly trained, I reckon.' He drew in a shivery breath. 'He ain't going to keep me, Rose. Waste of food.'

'You don't know that,' Freddie argued.

'What would he want me for?' Bill muttered. 'I'm no magician, and I ain't going to join their gang, not that I should think they'd trust me to, anyway. He'll do what he did with Eliza.'

'No, he won't,' Rose snarled, like a vicious little cat. She sprang up, her fists clenched. She had been feeling hopeless, sick with fright. Beset with so much awfulness that she didn't know what to do first, she was doing nothing, and simply trying not to howl. But she was not going to let anyone drown her Bill. 'Three magicians. We can't be this feeble. We have to be able to get ourselves out, there's only one of him, and frankly, he can't be that clever, or he'd be an awful lot better known.'

'What I keep thinking is, why aren't they richer?'

179

Freddie muttered. 'I suppose they have to keep hidden, but this place is falling apart.'

'Don't you think his magic is odd?' Rose asked. 'I've never seen magic so obviously all over someone before. Usually you have to look so hard.' She frowned. 'And he hit you, Freddie, really hit you, I mean, not with a spell. Why would he do that? Perhaps he isn't as strong as he looks.'

'There's your mother too,' Bella said hesitantly.

Rose nodded. 'I know. She's forced to work for him, though. If we could break the spell, I know she would come with us. She wanted to, didn't she? I know she raised the alarm, but I don't think he could actually make her do anything to hurt us. He's on his own. And his gang are idiots.'

'Rather large idiots,' Freddie muttered.

'But not the slightest bit powerful, if we could use our magic,' Rose reminded him.

'We're stuck in here, though, ain't we?' Bill was looking at her with just the slightest hint of hope in his eyes now. 'Can't fight from behind these walls.'

Rose frowned. There had to be a way – the things she had seen Freddie do, in their lessons with Mr Fountain – and she was supposed to be as powerful as he was, just not as practised. Let alone how strong Bella was. She had believed they were stuck when Miss Sparrow had imprisoned them in a stone cellar underground, but there was no stone here, no solid walls, only a battered old boat. Surely it couldn't hold them?

But they hadn't got any further towards an escape plan by the time Bella gave up and fell asleep against Rose's shoulder.

'They're leaving us to stew for the night,' Bill reckoned. 'They'll roust us out early in the morning, when we're really scared. We should all try and sleep. No point lying awake and worrying.'

It was easy to say. But Rose leaned against the wooden wall, her arms prickly with the slumped weight of Bella, and thought about her mother.

By the next morning, Freddie's longing for crumpets had spread to everyone, and they still couldn't think of a way to get out. Bella was getting more fractious and difficult by the minute, and Rose was beginning to wonder if perhaps they should encourage her. If they could stand the agony and bleeding ears, perhaps Bella could scream their way out? She would surely be able to break down the boat timbers.

Freddie lifted the marble up, looking around their prison. 'You know, we've only tried getting out of the trapdoor. I wonder if his spell goes all the way round.' He climbed up onto the old box he'd been sitting on, and peered at the timbers. 'It feels very old, this boat. Maybe it's not too solid.'

Rose knocked against the nearest wall, and sighed with frustration. 'It feels solid. Heavy.' She remembered the mast, back in Dover harbour, and sighed. Her magic hadn't worked then either. But she knocked at the wall again, more thoughtfully, and then pressed her hands against it, flat-palmed, feeling the wood, and remembering the water, crumpling against the harbour wall.

'What's the matter? Have you found a weak point?' Freddie asked eagerly, and Bill stood up to see what she was doing.

'No... But I can feel the sea.'

'Rose, it's a river we're next to. The Thames.'

Rose rolled her eyes at Freddie, and stroked the timbers again. 'It remembers the sea, Freddie. I don't think it likes being run aground.'

'Someone's coming!' Bella said sharply, and Rose jumped down. Freddie blew on the marble and stuffed it into his pocket, and they tried to look cowed and sad and not as though as they were considering escape at all.

The hatch creaked and whined as it was wrenched open, and Rose tried to see the spell as it died away, but she couldn't get a grip on it. Pike hung over the doorway, looking fox-like and pleased with himself, and Rose thought again that his magic didn't seem to fit. Could he have stolen it somehow? Most of the magicians she had met inhabited their magic like a well-made suit of clothes. It moved with them. They belonged in it. Pike seemed to use his instead, picking it up and throwing it at people. She was almost sure he was not a natural magician. It would explain why he had had to steal Miranda.

However, even if the magic wasn't his, he used it very well. She tried pushing against it with the merest feather-light touch of her own magic as he dropped gracefully into the room, and he swung round and smiled at her at once. 'Be careful, girl. I'm still watching, and two of my men are up there, ready to nab slippery little children.' His smile grew wider. 'I only came to see if you would like to visit your mother.' His voice was a purr, and Rose flinched away from it. She looked helplessly between Bill and Bella and Freddie. What should she do? Of course she wanted to, but was this some sort of trap?

Bill shook his head slightly, and Rose could see that he thought they should stay together.

'May we all go?' she asked, trying to sound polite, while her fingers curled into furious little claws.

Pike stared at her blankly. 'No.'

'Then I won't.'

He blinked, as though he simply couldn't believe that she had just denied him. Rose supposed not that many people did.

'Be careful,' Bill breathed behind her. 'I think he's crazed.'

Rose was quite sure he was right. It was something about Pike's pale, pale eyes. They were unstable. He clambered back out of the trapdoor, and it slammed shut, shaking the whole boat-room, and making Bella squeal.

Freddie began to mutter worriedly about whether it had been wise to upset Pike, but Rose was standing in the centre of the tiny room, her arms outstretched, smiling to herself.

'What is it?' Freddie demanded, pulling out the glowing marble. 'What have you done?'

'He let it go. His magic. And now it's high tide,' Rose told him dreamily. 'Can't you feel it pulling? When Pike slammed the trapdoor, he hit the boat with all that furious magic, all loose. He likes to bind things together, like he bound my mother, and that magic wanted to cling on to something. I'd spoken to the wood already, and it was waiting.'

Freddie grabbed her shoulders. 'Rose, *what have you done?*'

184

'It isn't me, it's the boat.'

Bill frowned. 'There ain't a boat, Rose. Just the beaten-up old bits of one. It ain't going anywhere.'

Rose smiled. 'It thinks it is.' She could feel the boat now, straining at a mooring rope, its old, dull-red, gaff-rigged sail starting to swell and fill and flap. 'It can feel the water, and it wants to be gone. A little bit of my spells, from when I wanted to get out, and a lot of Pike's loose magic. Now the boat wants to escape too…'

The little room shook suddenly, and Bill sat down, his eyes panicky. 'Rose, this ain't a boat, you can't sail off in nothing and old wood!'

Bella patted his knee. 'She likes sea journeys. She invented one inside my head a few days ago. If she says there's a boat, there probably is.'

'There's boats and boats. I bet it's got holes in,' Bill muttered.

Freddie snickered, sharp and hysterical. 'It's all hole!'

Then there was a splintering, crashing explosion of sound, and they shot forwards, grabbing onto each other, and yelling in fear and joy and excitement.

The half-boat flung itself against the stones of the outer wall, and as they broke out of the warehouse, Rose felt Pike's magic tearing away, like an ugly coat of slime. There was a sickening lurch as they slipped over the little causeway, and then smoothness, as the water sucked at the strange memory of a boat. The timbers quivered with their new-found freedom, and Bill reached up to the hatch. 'Can't get to it. Climb on my shoulders?'

Freddie nodded, and scrambled up, shoving hard with his hands flattened against the boards. 'It's still bolted, but his spell's half torn off. Can you hold me up here a minute?'

'Mmpf,' Bill muttered. 'Hurry up.'

Freddie drew a series of interlocking patterns on the underside of the hatch, and then swept his hand across them. Then he shoved again, and cried out gleefully as the hatch sprang open. His head and shoulders disappeared out of the hole, and then he called down to Bill. 'Push me out, then I can pull you all up.'

Bill boosted him out, then stood on one of the boxes to make it easier for Freddie to haul him up, and then they dragged the girls out of the hatch, Bella kicking and yelping indignantly. They huddled together up on the bows, staring back into the well of the boat.

'Oh…' Rose gazed around them, wide-eyed.

'Mmm. Imaginary boat,' Freddie agreed. 'I'd never have believed it.'

'Not completely imaginary,' Bella disagreed. 'I can

see it. Can't you? Just very faintly?'

The bow of the fishing vessel, the part they had been imprisoned in, looked like any old boat, although very worn and battered. But the rest of the boat was – not there. Or almost there, as Bella said, one could see it very faintly, a honey-golden haze of new timber – there was even a sweetish whiff of cut wood. And it was sailing, wallowing through the wide, pewter-grey river.

'Do you think we can touch the rest of the boat?' Freddie asked. 'I mean, would it hold us? I don't feel very safe clinging on up here.'

Bill snorted. 'It don't look very safe down there. I'm staying where I can see the wood. No offence, Rose. But I can only see water down there, and it looks cold.'

'They've seen us.' Rose had been staring back towards the old Beloveds warehouse, watching for Pike. He was easy enough to spot, even from this distance, his hair a flaming spot of red against the tumbled grey stones. The rest of the gang were gathered around him, pointing. There was a small rowing boat, tied to a metal ring on the wall, but no one seemed to be about to give chase.

Rose sighed, and looked away, out to the other side of the river. The warehouses were shrouded in early-morning mist, but there was the odd boat busy ploughing up the river already, and their occupants

187

were staring at the strange little craft.

'We should make for the bank again. Try and moor somewhere further down, away from Beloveds, and then we can get back,' she suggested.

'Back?' Bella squeaked. 'We aren't going back! We've just got away.'

Rose nodded. 'That's all right. You can go home. I'm going back.'

Freddie rubbed a hand across his face. 'Sorry, Rose. I'd almost forgotten why we went there in the first place. Your mother's still there.'

'And I should think Pike will take it out on her that he's lost us,' Rose said quietly. 'We've only made things worse for her.'

'No.' Another voice joined in, and the children wriggled round to face the well of the boat, where a silvery figure was watching them, as insubstantial as the timbers she stood on.

'Eliza! We didn't know if you'd come back!' Rose frowned. 'Be careful, won't you? We don't know what that part of the boat actually is.'

Eliza smiled. 'I'm not afraid of getting wet, Rose. Besides, it feels solid to me. I've seen your mother, Rose. I went back. She saw me, too, or she almost did. Pike tried to cripple her with the spell, but it didn't take this time. She's growing away from him – you broke

188

his hold on her, Rose. She's happy.'

'Can she get away?' Rose demanded.

Eliza shook her head. 'No. He still has her bound, but I think her real magic was waking up inside her again. I don't know how much longer his spell will hold.'

Rose laughed. 'But then we did it! We've freed her. If Pike's spell is wearing off, she'll be able to get away!'

Eliza was silent for a moment, staring down at the strange floor of the boat, her wet hair trailing over her face.

'What is it?' Rose asked uncertainly. 'What's wrong?'

'Pike knows too. He can tell he's losing her.' Eliza looked up, shaking her hair back. 'He'll kill her first. He could do that, now, while he still has her just enough under his control. He can't let her escape. She'd have the law after him, and if they knew what they were fighting, if she told them how to fight him, he knows he wouldn't have a chance. He doesn't want to be hanged, Rose.'

Rose laughed bitterly. 'So she's going to die happy, that's what you meant by us not making things worse? We have to go back and get her.' She smacked the roof of the cabin angrily. 'How do we make this thing move? We need to turn around.'

'It's partly made of your magic, I should think you

189

just tell it.' Freddie reached out to touch the side of the boat, his fingers stroking the hardly-there wood. 'It feels like you, Rose. You and the memories in the wood, that's all.'

'Look!' Bill nudged them both. 'That cat, running along the slipway there. Is that Himself?'

Freddie peered across the water. 'I think so. Gus! Gus, we're here!'

'I can see you, you idiot,' came a mewing cry across the water. 'Why else would I be down by the river on a freezing February morning?'

'Is the master with you?' Freddie called back, ignoring the insults, which was second nature by now.

Gus shook his head. 'Stuck at the palace.' His whiskers were bristling with tiny, silvery sparks, Rose noticed, frowning. The white cat often glittered when he was working a spell, but this looked different. Gus was worried, and trying not to show it. She had a dreadful feeling that she knew why. Her mouth was suddenly full of a strange, bitter taste of dismay.

'The Talish invasion is about to begin, according to some intelligence the king had smuggled out. They're preparing to embark, and Aloysius is desperately trying to gather everyone together to fight.' Gus's tail swished anxiously. 'I decided I'd better save you myself, since we ought to get back and help. Although you seem to have saved yourselves without me, which is most ungracious.'

Their odd craft had turned, with a great creaking of phantom sails, and was now cutting through the water towards Gus's slipway.

'Did you tell it to do that?' Bill asked, impressed.

'Not really. It just did. I suppose I hadn't told it anywhere I wanted it to go before, so it was just going. Now it knows we want to be over there.'

There was a certain smugness about the sails, as the boat drew up alongside the wooden slipway, where Gus was sitting, staring down at them disapprovingly.

'Really. An imaginary boat? Could you not manage something better?'

'It's getting more real, I think,' Rose noted, as they scrambled off onto the slipway. She held out her hand to Eliza, who was hesitating over the band of dark water between the boat and the wooden boards. 'I won't let you fall in it,' she whispered. She knew that Eliza couldn't drown again, and so did the ghost, but the water was as dark and thick and sucking as treacle. Eliza gripped Rose's hand with her own chill fingers, and jumped, her eyes closed in fear. Then she scurried along the slipway towards the solid stone walls of another tumbledown warehouse.

'Look, you can see proper wood, almost.' Rose

kneeled down and stroked the honey-yellow wood gently. 'Where will you go now?' she whispered, and felt the boat rock excitedly under her fingers. She smiled. 'Good luck, wherever you are.'

'Do you think a strange boat is just going to turn up in someone's mooring?' Bill asked, watching it shear off into the wind.

Rose smiled. 'One that always seems to weather the storms better than anyone else's. It's a good boat. They'd better look after it.' She stared fiercely across the water as the boat seemed to melt into the dancing February sun. Then she shook herself, and turned to Gus.

'Listen, my mother is still in the warehouse. We escaped by accident, we didn't really plan, and so…'

'Oh good.' Gus's whiskers perked up a little. 'I was beginning to think you had managed that without me, which would have been disappointing. So we have to go back and rescue her.'

Rose nodded. 'How did you get away before? Did you find a different way out? We didn't see.'

Gus snorted delicately. 'Of course you didn't. When Miranda began to raise the alarm I shot out into the passageway and back the way we'd come. It was fairly obvious you idiots weren't going to get out in time – no point in all of us being caught.'

Freddie rolled his eyes. 'Always heroic.'

Gus simply yawned, showing all his sparkling teeth. 'I'm here, aren't I? For the actually dangerous and difficult part. All you managed to do was get out. You need me to do anything useful.'

Rose put a hand in front of Freddie, who was starting to seethe. 'Don't, Freddie. We haven't time to fight. Gus, Eliza thinks Pike is going to kill my mother so she can't escape.'

Gus nodded brightly. 'A challenge, then. What do we know about this Pike?'

'Well, he's mad.' Freddie shrugged. 'That's about it.'

'I don't think he understands how to use the magic properly,' Rose said slowly. 'He seems to just – fling it about... Gus, could he have stolen it? Could he have a thing, a talisman, like the mask that Gossamer stole? And it's that that gives him the magic? He seems very, very strong, but not quite right, somehow.'

Freddie frowned. 'Oh. I thought that was just because he was mad.'

'It's how the boat happened, I think. When he was angry that I wouldn't do as he said, the magic got loose, and because my magic was already in the boat timbers, it followed it there...'

Bill frowned. 'If half his magic's just sailed off down the river, does that mean he isn't a magician any more?

Did you steal his power, Rosie?'

Rose longed to say yes, but she looked doubtfully at Gus and Freddie and Bella, and shook her head. 'It'll grow again, won't it? Do you think?'

Gus nodded. 'But the boy is right. That could take time. We should hurry, while we might still have an advantage.'

Freddie folded his arms. 'It's all very well saying hurry. What are we hurrying *to*? We don't have a plan – we can't just walk in and ask for her back.'

Gus smiled a cat smile, his eyes narrowing in pleasure. 'Actually, I thought that's exactly what I might do. Walk, boy, and listen.'

They set off, hurrying down the slipway to solid ground, and following Gus through a series of dark, winding alleys.

'Pike may be a magician, but the rest of the gang are not, hmmm?' Gus explained as they scurried after him. 'And he is weakened at the moment, or so we hope. So if we stay out of his way, we should be able to do this with a relatively simple series of spells.'

'Don't we need to go this way?' Bill asked, pointing down a dark passage, the roofs of the warehouses almost touching overhead. 'We want to get back to the water, don't we? So we can find the hole the boat made.'

'Too obvious,' Freddie disagreed. 'They'll be expecting that, it'd be guarded.'

'And the front won't?' Bill folded his arms disgustedly and stared down at Freddie.

'Shut up!' Gus hissed. 'We don't have time for this. Where's that ghost-girl gone?'

Eliza, who had been lurking behind Rose, shuffled forwards a little. Rose frowned. Was Gus hoping to use her to get them inside? She wasn't sure it would work. Eliza seemed so fragile, and it was obviously hard for her to control how she moved outside the mirror.

'What sort of things was Pike involved in, when you lived there? Extortion? Gambling? Robbery?' Gus demanded.

Eliza nodded. 'All of that. But he got a lot of his money off the protection racket. He only had to look at a grate and the fire would start burning – it persuaded people pretty well.'

'What does she mean?' Bella whispered to Rose.

'I think people paid him not to burn down their shops,' Rose told her, shuddering.

Bella looked intrigued. 'How clever.'

'Bella!'

'Well, it is. To have people paying you not to do things. It sounds ideal.'

Gus prowled on, the tip of his tail twitching

195

thoughtfully. 'So if a boy came to them, looking for a reward… Perhaps he was wanting to tell them about a new grocer's opening, not too far away – just far enough to be into the respectable streets, they'd let him in – right through their front entrance. And really, once one of us is in, it should be no trouble at all to open a door to the rest, especially as Pike might be indisposed.'

Rose frowned. 'I suppose we know where my mother is, now. She knows we might come back, too. She'd be ready, perhaps. She could help us to set her free.'

'You've forgotten something,' Freddie pointed out gloomily.

Gus pricked his ears up curiously.

'This boy who's got to get us in. They know what I look like, Gus. They aren't going to let me anywhere. Unless we do a glamour, and that takes ages to get right. We aren't all as good at it as Rose's mother.'

Gus sighed. 'I wasn't talking about you, dear boy. I meant me.'

Eliza hissed loudly in Rose's ear. 'But he's a cat!'

'That's what you think,' Gus spat irritably, and he disappeared behind a rickety iron staircase. When he came back, he was a boy about the same age as Freddie, with similar whitish-blonde hair – but unlike

Freddie's, it looked grubby and uncombed, and he was wearing scruffy trousers, and a jacket with patches. Only his eyes were the same as before – one amber, one blue, and both sparkling evilly.

Rose stared at him. She had seen Gus as a boy once before, in Venice, but only behind a mask. This was the first time she had seen his human face. He had a very pointed chin, and his eyes were rather round and set far apart like a cat's, but that was the sort of thing you only noticed if you knew.

'Hello, Rose,' he purred, and she jumped, realising how rude it was to stare so. Bill was scowling, which Gus seemed to think was very funny. He kept chuckling to himself. But at last they rounded a corner, and he held up one finger to shush everyone. 'Look, there's the warehouse. Stay here. I'll call you once I'm past the guards, if the story works.'

'What if it doesn't?' Rose murmured anxiously. Gus as a boy didn't have the same air of unshakeable confidence as he did when he was a cat.

He sighed at her. 'Well, then I won't.' And he sauntered off up the alleyway with his paws – hands – in his pockets.

They sat hidden behind a pile of old packing cases, watching the door of the warehouse anxiously.

197

'He's been a very long time,' Freddie muttered. 'We should have made him take Eliza, then at least he'd have more idea where he was going.'

Bella scowled. 'This coat is ruined.'

Rose!

Rose sat up sharply. 'Freddie, that wasn't you, was it?'

'No! Did he call you?'

'I think so…'

Of course I did, idiot! Come on, there's not a lot of time. I've sent the two men by the door to sleep, so you can sneak in, but I can feel Pike's magic, and he's getting stronger again.

'I hope he's right about this,' Bill growled, as they peered round the shabby door to the warehouse. 'I don't like just walking in the front door.'

'Stop complaining.' Rose took hold of Bella's hand, and dragged her into the shadowy building. The front part was simply a cavernous warehouse, piled with boxes and barrels. The two sleeping guards were collapsed on a pile of oriental carpets, which looked quite valuable.

Gus was beckoning to them from the other side of the space, by a small door. 'It's this way,' he whispered, as soon as they reached him. 'I got to her room, but I think it'll need all of us to break Pike's spell – you

198

especially, Rose. And once we start to try, he'll know what we're doing, and he'll come running.'

'Leave me here, outside her door,' Eliza whispered. 'I'll warn you if he's coming.'

This time, Miranda wasn't hopelessly facing the wall. She was still sitting on the bed, but she was staring intently at the door, as though she had been waiting for them to arrive. Her eyes were bright with hope and excitement, and as soon as she saw Rose, she tried to leap to her feet.

'Ah! I can't.' She held her hands at her sides, squeezing her fingers into painful fists. 'I'm holding back the alarm spell, but I can't do it for long. He'll be here. Please, help me break the binding.'

'Do you know how he set it?' Freddie asked, kneeling beside her.

She shook her head. 'No. Except that he's been adding to it for years – like layers and layers of silken ropes tying me down. There must be a way for someone to slice through them.'

Gus sat down on the bed beside her, and stretched out one finger. His nails were slightly hooked, like claws. He pulled at the air around Miranda, and made a spitting sound. 'Tight,' he muttered. 'Nothing to get a grip on.'

Rose's mother gave him an odd look, and Rose

explained hastily. 'He's a cat.'

'Oh! What a remarkable transformation.'

Gus grinned at her, showing off all his teeth, which were still very sharp.

Rose stroked her mother's arm. 'I can hardly feel the spell,' she confessed. Her fingers were tingling, but it was with excitement, not magic.

Miranda smiled. 'Keep doing that. I'm sure it's weakening, even if you're doing it by accident. And if it doesn't work, at least I'll remember you doing it. But promise me, if he comes, you'll run, all of you. You have to leave me here.'

Rose frowned. She wasn't sure she could promise. But Bella nodded. 'We'll make her go. We promise.'

'You need to cut the spell away.' Eliza had appeared beside her, and now she whispered in Rose's ear.

'I'll go and take over watching,' Bill muttered.

Rose turned to see the silver ghost hovering shyly next to her. 'How? Do you know how we do it, Eliza?'

'She is here, then!' Rose's mother exclaimed. 'I thought I'd seen her.'

'Yes, Miss Miranda. Sorry, miss,' Eliza whispered.

'She's sorry – about taking the mirror,' Rose explained.

Her mother shook her head. 'After everything she did, she's no need to say sorry. She saved you, Hope, she was the one who got you away from this awful place. How did you find her?'

'She's in your mirror,' Rose explained, pulling it out of the inside of her coat. 'Because she took it, she's haunted it ever since.'

'The mirror will break the spell,' Eliza breathed in her ear, her breath frosty-cold. 'If you break the mirror. Then use the largest shard of the mirror-glass to cut away the spell-bindings.'

Rose stared at her. 'Really? And then she'll be free?'

Eliza nodded. 'Powerful spell, that mirror, miss.'

Rose drew in one delighted breath to tell the others, but then she frowned, turning back to the ghost-child. 'Eliza, what happens to you if I break the mirror?'

Eliza smiled faintly. 'Nothing.'

Rose stared at her. 'You're sure?'

'Oh yes.'

Rose held the mirror by the handle, and stared around. There was nothing to break it with.

'Stamp on it,' Eliza hissed. 'Put it on the floor and stamp on it.'

Rose nodded, and raised the heel of her boot to crush the glass. She was looking at Eliza as she did it, and she saw the strangest expression cross her silver-mist face – a mixture of pain, and relief, and a sort of pleased surprise. And then she was gone.

Rose looked around, expecting her to reappear somewhere else in the room, but she didn't. Her mother twisted painfully inside her spell-bindings, and Rose heard her whisper, 'Oh, Liza...' Her voice quivered and cracked.

'She's not coming back,' Gus said, with a certain satisfaction.

Rose turned on him. 'You knew, didn't you?'

'Knew what?' Gus asked innocently.

'That she'd go! I shouldn't have believed her, she said nothing would happen.'

'Rose, she was telling the truth,' Gus told her, gripping her hand. She was sure she could feel fur between her fingers. 'That's what she meant. Nothing happened to her. That's what she is now.'

'I didn't know she meant it like that,' Rose whispered, stricken.

'Don't waste what she did for you,' Gus reminded her. 'It only worked because she gave herself up. She knew what she was doing, Rose. She'd sacrificed herself to save you once before, remember. And now we haven't much time.'

Rose nodded, and wiped her hand across her eyes to brush the tears away. She looked down at the mirror glass, broken into lethal shards.

'Hit it on the floor! Quickly!' Bella muttered. 'Look,

I don't think she can keep the alarm spell under control for much longer.'

Rose glanced up at her mother anxiously. She was biting into her lip, and her eyes were squeezed tight shut. Sharply, Rose hit the boarded floor with the mirror, and lifted the frame away, leaving the shattered glass on the floor. She picked up the largest, sharpest piece, and turned to her mother. 'Where do I cut?' she asked helplessly.

'I doubt it matters,' Gus told her. 'Be quick!'

'Oh, Eliza, please make this work,' Rose begged, and she sliced quickly across her mother's golden-bronze hair – it seemed the only safe place, although a great pity to cut off such pretty hair.

But the hair didn't come off. Instead a sticky, translucent mass like snail slime seemed to appear for a second, then melt away. Her mother sprang up, and hugged her, and then whispered, 'Run!'

TEN

They all piled out into the passageway, and Rose looked from side to side in dismay. She had no idea which way to go, and now they hadn't Eliza to guide them. Gus slipped past her, and stood scenting the air. Rose was sure she could see his whiskers, despite his human shape.

'Gus sent the guards at the front to sleep – is that the best way out?' she asked her mother quickly.

Miranda shook her head. 'I have no idea. I've never been out of that room. But – no. Pike is coming that way. I can feel him, like some great wounded slug, drenched in poison. This way, towards the water, come on.'

There was shouting now at the end of the

passageway, and Gus hissed. 'I missed those.' His fingernails had grown even longer, and his front teeth were cat-like and sharp.

'You'll get your chance,' Miranda said, not looking back at him. 'Is this where you broke out this morning? Good gracious, Hope, what did you do?'

'Rose,' Bill snapped. 'She isn't Hope, she's Rose. I know it weren't your fault she got left, but she did, and she's Rose now.'

Miranda looked stricken, but she nodded. 'I'm sorry. Later, we can talk about these things.'

Rose smiled. 'Not now.' She gazed, rather proudly, at the enormous hole in the wall. 'We enlivened half a boat,' she explained, 'and sailed it away. Through there.' It was the *largest* thing she had ever seen her magic do, and she was quite pleased with it.

'They'll not have left this unguarded,' Bill muttered, looking around suspiciously. 'Where are they... Oh, blast...'

A tall, chronically thin man had materialised from the shadows, wielding a knife, and he was holding it at Bella's throat. Her eyes were bulging, and she was holding her breath, trying to make herself as thin as possible to escape the blade.

'Where was he?' Freddie muttered. 'How did we miss him?'

205

'The others are coming...' Bill was staring behind them. 'Or at least, someone is. I think it's Pike, but he looks – different.'

'We stole a lot of his magic for the boat.' Rose was still staring at Bella. Why didn't she scream? When they got home, Miss Fell was going to have to stop teaching them etiquette and work out how Bella could control her screaming trick so it only hit the right people.

Rose smiled grimly to herself. When. Not if.

The thin man was shaking, they could all see the blade wavering against Bella's skin.

'He's drugged,' Bill muttered.

Miranda nodded. 'They trade in opium. They tried to give it to me once.'

There was the faintest squeak, and a thin red line appeared across Bella's neck. The thin man laughed. 'Master's coming...'

Pike had dragged himself up the passageway. His skin was greyish, and his mouth looked wet, as though he'd been drooling. He moved as though he was having to think about every lurching step, but the madness was still there in his pale eyes, and somehow he seemed even more dangerous than before. His eyes were paler now, the pupils shrunk to the merest pinpricks, leaving that flat expanse of blue.

Rose and her mother and Bill and Freddie were

206

pressed up against the edges of the hole in the wall, close enough to jump through and run, but they couldn't leave Bella.

'Go!' Rose hissed to her mother.

'I can't leave you all!'

'You tried to make me promise I would. It's you he wants back. Run!'

Miranda laughed. 'I think he'd rather have all three of you. Young and strong, you're exactly what he needs. I'm not going, not without the little one. Hold hands with me, Rose. We're going to get her back.'

The china-whiteness of her face was flushing slowly pinker, and she seemed to be growing more alive every minute. Her hair was crackling with energy, and even her dingy greyish dress was a taking on a silvery lustre of heavy silk.

Pike was watching her, grinding his teeth. 'There's your escape.' He nodded at the gaping hole in the wall. 'But you can't go,' he snarled. 'You won't leave the child…' He sounded doubtful.

'You're right. You would, but then you are a thief and a child-murderer. I'll never forget what you did to Eliza, and what you made me do to my baby.' Rose's mother seemed to be growing taller as she hurled the words at him, and Pike was cowering backwards. 'Your magic isn't even your own to use,' Miranda snarled,

207

and then she laughed as Pike cried out in horror. 'Did you think I didn't know? I saw it in you years ago. All stolen. The very first thing you stole, and from your own brother. You stole his magic, Jonathan Fisher, and that was all it was ever good for, for stealing more things.'

Pike sat down suddenly, as though someone had sliced across the backs of his knees. 'You know my name.'

'And Jacob's. The brother you killed.' Miranda nodded, but behind her back she was pulling Bill's sleeve, pointing him towards the thin man and Bella.

'I didn't! I didn't kill him!' Pike screamed. 'I didn't. He's over there, look at him!'

Startled, they looked across at the thin, shaking man, and saw that he had red hair too, under the layers of dirt. He was staring back, looking frightened, and his hands were shaking even more. He wasn't looking at Bella.

Miranda glanced between the two of them. 'You drugged him, then. So you could take his power. You really are a slug. Was that why you tried to get me to take the stuff? So that you could steal my magic for ever too?' She shuddered. 'Was it what you were planning for these three?'

'No one's stealing anything from me!' Bella suddenly

screamed, as she stamped her pretty high-heeled boot down on Jacob Fisher's foot. Gus leaped from behind him to rake his claws across the man's face, and Bill snatched Bella as she ducked out of his grip, and bundled her through the hole in the wall, grabbing Freddie's arm and dragging him after them. 'Come on, Rose!'

Rose pulled her mother's hand, and they scrambled over the rubble, leaving Jacob moaning behind them, and Pike dragging himself in their wake, as they raced along the narrow stone pathway that ran around the crumbling warehouse, a ribbon of safety between the walls and the water.

When they were back at the mouth of the alley, Rose threw her arms around Bella, the scarlet line across Bella's pretty throat filling her with fury. She had never thought she would want to kill anyone. She had hated and suppressed and fought against her magic, but now she would never give it up. Pike had stolen it once before by taking her mother and her history away from her, and now he was planning to steal it again.

'Bella, could you scream that building down?'

Bella nodded, her teeth showing in an angry little smile. She had wiped her nice glove across the cut, and she was staring at the stain. 'But won't it hurt you all?'

Rose shook her head. 'Not if we're in the hiding spell first, I hope. We never tried to ward it off before.'

'Take hands,' Gus snapped. His bloodstained claws had retracted into normal fingernails again as he stretched his hands out to the others. 'The strongest you've ever done the spell.'

The shimmering bubble wrapped them all, leaving Bella standing alone in front of them.

'I can't do it,' she muttered. 'I've never done it on purpose!' She looked round at Rose, her face panicky.

'He's coming!' Freddie yelped, pointing at the gap in the stone wall, and Bella wheeled around and screamed out of pure terror, a wave of sound that the others felt even inside their protection spell, battering and swinging against the stone walls and their own fragile wall of magic.

'He wasn't coming,' Gus muttered to Freddie, and Freddie shook his head. 'But he would have been in a minute. She needed scaring into it.'

Bella jumped back suddenly, the scream dying away into a yelp of fright, as the building seemed to shimmer. 'It's pulling me in,' she gasped, her lace-edged skirts suddenly sucking towards the warehouse. As the others broke out of the disguise spell and seized her, they felt as though a strong wind was sweeping them back towards the crumbling stones of Beloveds.

Rose's mother stood there, her feet planted on the stones, her long, bronze-gold hair streaming out past her face towards the old warehouse. She had grabbed Bella's coat, hauling her back like a sailor rescuing a man overboard. 'Hold on to her,' she hissed through her clenched teeth to Rose, Bill and Freddie, and she stood like a rock, her face growing impossibly whiter, until the warehouse seemed all at once to sink into itself, leaving a cloud of choking dust.

The last shreds of the disguise spell faded away, and they stared gaping at the devastation.

'He's gone,' someone whispered, and Rose found that she was holding her mother's hand.

They straggled back through the dirty alleys, gradually reaching the smarter, cleaner streets, but there was still a curious air of desolation. Hardly anyone was about, although it was mid-morning now, and those people who were out were hurrying, heads down with anxious faces.

'Something's happened,' Freddie muttered, walking faster.

'It has to be the invasion. There must have been news.' Gus was a cat again, dancing ahead of their feet, and sniffing the air luxuriously. No one cared enough to be surprised by him right now.

211

'But Papa was going to stop it!' Bella murmured anxiously. 'It can't be.'

'Who are we invading?' Rose's mother asked, and they stared at her.

She sighed. 'Eleven years – no one talked to me.'

'Talis is invading *us*,' Rose explained. 'Or they were going to. Bella's father went to the palace – yesterday? The day before? I can't think.'

'The day before.' Bella's hands were clenched inside her bloodstained gloves. 'What if he's hurt?'

Gus suddenly stopped, and turned back to them, his tail swishing in agitation. 'We've been gone overnight.'

Rose and the others nodded, unsure what he meant.

'Don't you see?' Gus snarled. 'The one thing guaranteed to draw Aloysius away from the war committee. Bella, and you two, gone. He'll be back at the house, searching. We have to run!'

'Oh no,' Rose muttered, starting to dash after him, pulling her mother with her, and all six of them raced through the streets, back to the tall house in the square.

Freddie hammered on the front door, and it opened so suddenly that Rose was sure Mr Fountain had been pacing the hallway, waiting for them.

'You're safe!' He caught Bella up in his arms. 'I heard you screaming.'

'She collapsed a warehouse, sir!' Freddie told him.

 212

'On purpose,' he added quickly. 'We needed her to.'

But Mr Fountain had seen Rose's mother, standing nervously in the doorway with Rose still clinging to her hand.

'Rose?' He looked at them both, frowning. 'Who...'

'Miranda!' Miss Fell was hurrying down the stairs, her stick forgotten, a new life in her face. 'Oh, Rose, you found her!'

Mr Fountain swallowed. 'Miranda *Fell*?'

'Miranda Garnet.' Rose's mother's voice was proud, and her shoulders were unyieldingly stiff, as her aunt embraced her.

'Miranda, where have you been? I shall never, ever forgive you for going off without telling me!' Miss Fell stared at her niece. 'Did you think I would disown you?' She stood holding Miranda, staring at every line of her face. 'Oh, my dearest. So changed. But then, eleven years, and it's seemed so much longer.'

Miss Bridges, the housekeeper, had appeared discreetly through the green baize door. 'Tea, ma'am?' she murmured, and Miss Fell nodded, towing Miranda after her into the drawing room, pushing her into one of the button-back velvet chairs, and simply staring at her.

Mr Fountain had followed them in, still holding Bella, who looked exhausted, and Rose and Freddie and Bill were lurking in the doorway.

'Come here, child!' Miss Fell commanded, beckoning to Rose, and delicately kicking a footstool towards Miranda's chair. 'Sit there. I want to see you together.'

Her cheeks burning, Rose did as she was told. She felt as though she was sitting for a portrait, like the handsome oil painting of Bella as a baby with her mother that hung over the fireplace. The thin white hand that brushed her cheek and then settled cautiously on her shoulder was only part of the pose. Except that it was shaking.

Rose reached back, suddenly ashamed of her dry, stained hands, and held it, and felt it still, and heard her mother sigh.

Miss Fell stared at them, her eyes glittering and hungry. 'I was right. Ever since I saw you in Venice that day, Rose, running along the quay. I should never have doubted it – look at the pair of you! I told you, Rose, didn't I, that I thought I would have known if Miranda had died? You found her for me, after all this time…I should have trusted my instincts better.'

'Aunt, what is happening?' Miranda's voice was husky, as though she had hardly used it over the years. 'The streets were dead. Fear seems to be seeping into the air.'

'It's definite,' Mr Fountain said flatly. 'The Talish are bringing the invasion force to Cormanse. They've been constructing barges – dreadful, flimsy things, but then, they only have to make one journey. Now they're waiting for a clear day to make the crossing. February – stupid time to do it, of course. But the Talish emperor has his spies everywhere, and I think the agreement I made for the king in Venice wasn't as secret as it was meant to be. Clearly the emperor didn't want us having any extra help.'

Rose gasped. 'Sir, did we stop you fighting it? We had to go, I'm so sorry.'

Mr Fountain sighed, and sat down on one of the brocade sofas with Bella in his arms. 'I don't think it made much difference that I had to leave, Rose. I'd gathered as many magicians as I could – old friends – and we've managed to keep the channel too rough to cross. But we can't do that for ever. The Talish magicians are so strong, so many of them, and we're worn out.'

'You can't give up.' Freddie stared at him, horrified.

Mr Fountain smiled sadly. 'I'm not giving up, Freddie. I collapsed. Since Gossamer stabbed me, I don't have the same strength. They brought me home. Then when I got back here I discovered that you were all missing. Since then I've been trying to scry for you. I found you in some dank warehouse, but then you were on a boat – it was all muddled, and the wound kept making me lose the vision.' He hid his face in Bella's hair for a moment. 'I don't know if we can disturb the sea again.'

Miss Fell glared at him. 'Aloysius Fell, get up, and stop mooning about. Don't you realise what you have here?' She swept a hand around the drawing room. 'Three generations of the strongest magical talent in Europe. Plus Isabella, who may be objectionable, but is capable of screaming down buildings. And Frederick, who probably could too, if only he would make the effort.'

Freddie shrugged crossly, but Rose thought he was secretly rather pleased.

'Tell His Majesty that magicians cannot work in that dead stone monstrosity of a palace,' Miss Fell commanded. 'The sea spells are still working, are they not? The invasion cannot be for a few more days, surely?'

Mr Fountain shook his head dumbly.

'Then we must move somewhere more suitable. Your gathering of magicians from the palace, too.' She searched Miranda's face anxiously. 'Dearest, I must tell you…your parents…they died, a few years back.'

Miranda swallowed. 'I wondered,' she admitted.

'I don't know if I could have gone back and seen them, not even now.'

'The house will be yours,' her aunt pointed out gently. 'And Rose's.'

Gus mewed irritably. 'It won't be soon! A bunch of Talish officers will be using it for a billet if we don't do something!'

'Quite,' Miss Fell told him frostily. 'We need every advantage we can get, so the Fells will gather at Fell Hall. Miranda, you will have to be strong. Once this is all dealt with –' she waved a hand dismissively, and Rose had to stifle a little snort of laughter, for Miss Fell looked as though she was having problems with a lippy second footman, not an invasion – 'then you and Rose will be able to go wherever you like. But for now, we need the house on our side, my dear.'

Miranda nodded – and Rose noticed that her hand was shaking again.

Miss Fell stood up, in a grand sweep of stiff silk. 'William, send for the carriage, and tell the admirable Mrs Jones that we need provisions for a journey to Derbyshire.'

'So many of them…' Rose murmured, peering out of the carriage window. She and her mother were sharing a carriage with Miss Fell, and Gus, who had apparently abandoned his master for the sake of better gossip in Rose's party. 'They look exhausted already. They must have been marching for days.'

The column of soldiers stumbled past, their weapons jingling. But the polished swords were dusty, and the men themselves were no better. They hardly glanced up as the carriage sped past. 'Are they going to the coast?' Rose asked. 'In case – in case the plan doesn't work?'

Miss Fell nodded grimly. 'Or perhaps to the manufacturing towns. There are metalworks around here. It would be disastrous if the invading force should seize those.'

Rose watched the tail end of the dusty column disappearing behind them. They didn't look capable of defending a great deal. The plan had to work – or she could imagine the Talish forces simply sweeping their way across the country.

Miss Fell's determination that morning had seemed to fire Mr Fountain up. He'd slid Bella, who was now fast asleep, worn out by her destruction of the warehouse, off his shoulder, and lain her on the sofa, while he paced up and down the drawing room.

'You've never worked together, of course,' he'd muttered, suddenly glaring at Rose and her mother. 'And no time to test it. But three Fells, as you say...

Immensely powerful.' He stared at his perfectly shiny shoes for a few seconds, and glanced up. 'If we were to gather the whole invasion fleet close together – all those hundred barges that our agents have been gabbling in panic about – could you destroy them? With my help, and the other magicians I've recruited?'

Rose had simply stared at him, and then glanced up at her mother, and then her great-aunt, with her mouth half-open. But Miranda had wrinkled her nose and nodded, and Miss Fell had sniffed. 'Undoubtedly. Rose, well-bred young ladies do not sit around like frogs after flies. Close your mouth, dear.'

Mr Fountain had hared off to the palace without even putting on an overcoat, and demanded an immediate Council of War, at which he outlined the plan. It was a neat little trap, sending the major part of the British Navy off to rendezvous with the Venetians, and leaving the Channel hardly guarded. The Talish emperor and his generals would be forced to make a rather hasty decision. The whole invasion force, hopefully, would embark at once, straight into the hands of the waiting magicians.

It was all very well setting a trap – now Rose and the others had to spring it, and if they didn't, it wouldn't be a trap at all. It would simply be the most disastrous defeat. One that had been predicted by the Admiralty and the Horse Guards. Every senior military commander present at the king's council had threatened to leave the service, but as the king had declared that he was willing to entrust the fate of the nation to a handful of unreliable magic-workers holed up in a crumbling old house in the wilds of Derbyshire – as the First Lord of the Admiralty had put it before he actually did resign – there was very little they could do, short of forcing him to abdicate.

As the last jingling noises of the troops died away behind them, Rose shivered a little. The Talish soldiers probably wouldn't look so different. They would be tired too, after marching to Cormanse to embark on the barges. And they might well be seasick, some of them, perhaps even as bad as Bella.

It was the only thing that disturbed her about the plan. She was almost sure that Miss Fell was right, and they would be able to destroy the invasion force, even though she didn't feel like the blood of centuries of seers and mages was flowing through her veins, as Miss Fell had assured her it was. It would work. Hopefully.

But if it did, she would be as much a murderess as her mother.

*

'Rose, wake up.'

Someone was shaking her. Rose sat up, and winced. They had driven through the night, stopping only to change horses. She had been sleeping slumped against the someone's shoulder, she realised, and now she ached.

Her mother looked down at her, smiling a little. 'We're almost there, and it's getting light. So I thought you'd like to see...' She closed her eyes for a second. 'I wanted you to see it with me,' she added in a whisper.

Rose nodded, and crept one gloved hand around her mother's sleeve. She was wearing one of Miss Fell's travelling cloaks, a gloriously old-fashioned one with masses of capes around the collar, and a hat that trailed feathers. She looked very small and slight underneath it, and terribly frightened.

Miss Fell was glaring out of the carriage window – she was sitting facing the horses, of course. She had pulled an eyeglass out of her bag, and was examining the trees on either side of the drive.

'Bad pruning. Quite obvious. Really, I shall have to speak to Moffatt... And just look at those weeds in the drive!'

Rose thought it all looked immaculate, and she couldn't suppress a gasp as they finally drew up in the carriage circle in front of the house. She had seen it before, of course, but only in a painting, and that had been the terrace view. The front was even more impressive. The house was built of honey-coloured stone, not the gleaming white of the building she'd seen in the painting. The only thing that was familiar were the peacocks.

'This is the older part of the house,' Miss Fell explained, and even her voice had a slight crack to it, as though she too found it hard to be back. 'Built in the seventeenth century, by our ancestor, Richard Fell.'

Rose nodded. She wondered if he was the one Freddie had mentioned, and where he'd kept his dragon. The house looked as though it could house a whole colony of dragons – they could quite easily sleep in that little arched part over there. Rose blinked as they descended stiffly from the carriage, and the blinding winter sun seemed to catch a glinting scale, and perhaps a twitch of scaly claw. She really hadn't had a proper night's sleep, it was clear.

'I didn't believe I would ever come back.' Rose's mother was sitting on the marble terrace, with Rose beside her, both wrapped in layers of shawls. Rose kept looking around, frowning. It felt so very odd, as if she was inside that painting she had tried to copy. Or perhaps an illustration from a fairy tale, with the peacocks sweeping haughtily past.

'Are you happy – to be here?' she asked hesitantly.

Her mother stared out across the velvet green expanse of lawn. 'It's full of old ghosts. I'm not sure I could live here again.'

Rose nodded, a little relieved. They were still feeling their way around each other, but she supposed she belonged to her mother now. She knew she didn't want to live here either. She liked towns. The countryside was strangely empty, and still felt like something that ought to stay in pictures. The house itself was amazing, though – as steeped in spells as Mr Fountain's house, but about a hundred times larger and older. And she was almost sure the dragons had been true. She could *feel* them, something old and sly and wise that seemed to dart around the corners just ahead of her.

Freddie was finding it impossible to concentrate on the spells they were supposed to be planning. He kept disappearing on the way from one room to another, to be routed out an hour or so later by a polite servant, his eyes saucer-like, sure that he had only missed seeing one by inches.

Gus strolled up to Rose and her mother, leering at a nervous peacock, and leaped onto the arm of the bench.

'You should go back inside,' he yawned.

'Oh! Is it time?' Rose's heart thudded.

'Soon.'

In the drawing room behind them, there was a whispering of silk dresses and a smoothing of coat-tails, as forty people set down their afternoon teacups, and exchanged last nervous, encouraging glances.

Miss Fell's skeleton staff had risen to the challenge of their mistress and the cream of magical society descending on them for an unexpected house party. As Rose had suspected, the house was immaculate, and all the housekeeper had done when the news was broken to her was to purse her lips very slightly.

Miss Fell was sitting in a straight-backed wing chair, upholstered in purple damask, which had been placed just to the right of the fire. Mr Fountain was close by, and Miranda and the children were seated on stools around her. The other magicians were in chairs scattered throughout the room, but all facing Miss Fell, and close enough that everyone could clasp hands.

Rose could feel the ancient magic that filled every stone of the house. It whispered and called to her, stroking tiny fingers over her skin.

'Where are they now?' Mr Fountain asked a young man in a damson velvet jacket, with what Rose thought was a ridiculous mauve-spotted cravat. He was seated at a small wooden table with a map spread out in front

224

of him. One hand was laid flat on the map, and his eyes were half-closed.

'Here. Approaching Dover.'

'Are there balloons?' Bella asked, her high voice clearly audible in the nervous hush.

'Ssshh, Bella,' Rose and Freddie hissed, but the man in the velvet jacket laughed.

'No, that was only a rumour in the newspapers. The flotilla of barges only. The sea is very rough, the waves are almost swamping them already.'

'This is so risky,' a young woman seated close to Rose whispered. 'They should not have let them get this far. What if it goes wrong?'

Rose turned and glared at her, but she stared back hard-eyed, and Rose shivered. If it went wrong, they would have exposed England to a Talish invasion.

'Are they close enough together?' Rose's mother asked.

The velvet-jacket man nodded. 'Very close. It should work.'

It had been Rose and Freddie's idea to adapt Mr Fountain's protection spell into a trap for the invasion fleet, veiling them in a sudden, soundless bubble. Then the magicians together would drag the fleet under the waves, sinking it, and drowning the entire invading army. That part had made Rose run into the gardens to be sick in the shrubbery. Freddie had pointed out that it was only what the invasion force were intending to do to *them*, after all.

Rose could see his point, but it seemed so brutal. She had wanted to break the barges apart somehow, to at least give the soldiers a chance of being washed up onshore, and imprisoned.

No one else had agreed, and the half-retired admiral who was their liaison with the military forces had looked as though he wanted to slap her.

'Now.' The velvet-jacket man nodded, and everyone drew the symbols for the spell in the air, and then caught hands, to link the spell into a giant net.

Rose had never felt so much magic in one place before. She had never realised, but everyone's spells smelled different. Miss Fell's smelled of lavender, and Bella's of milk bonbons. Mr Fountain's reminded her of the pomade he applied to his moustache, and the man in the velvet jacket emitted a strong aroma of tobacco.

Her mother's smelled of dark sugar, from being imprisoned for so long in a cell made of black timbers from the hold of a ship. Rose closed her eyes, wrapped in lavender sugar, thinking of lavender glacé icing, and Mrs Jones's kitchen, and how her own unlikely story tied her to these two determined, impossible women.

The strength of the three of them was pulling the others out, over the odd calm of the sea.

It was as though she were being carried along on the waves of the spell, as they all streamed towards the invading ships. She could feel Bella beside her, clasping her hand tightly, and she knew that they were sitting on stools in the drawing room, but at the same time they were swooping and rushing through the air. Her hair was streaming behind her, and she laughed for joy at the feel of the wind in her face, a hundred times better than leaning over the side of a ship.

Then they drew close to the Talish barges, and the wonderful wind-rushing feeling died away, as she watched the men, ant-size in their dark-blue uniforms. How could she do this to them? She was quite sure that if King Albert had had half a chance he would have invaded Talis. These men were only doing what they were told. It simply wasn't fair. How could she have let them persuade her into this?

'We haven't a choice, Rose,' she felt her mother whisper in her ear.

'But it isn't fair. It's cruel. A hundred thousand men, they think!'

'It will end the possibility of the Talish invading.'

'We could do that just by destroying the ships,' Rose argued again. 'Those men would never let their commanders make them do it another time, would they?' Rose swallowed. 'If we do this, everyone will hate us. And they will be right.'

Her mother stared at her for a moment, and then Rose jumped as something patted her shoulder. Miss Fell had let go of Bella's other hand for long enough to tap Rose with the black lace fan looped around her wrist. 'Miranda, she's right. This is too much.' The old lady smiled, hawk-like. 'I have a solution. Remember all those times I made you unravel your crochet?'

Miranda wrinkled her nose. 'Can we unravel an invasion fleet?'

'My dear, you could unravel anything, you've had quite enough practice. If the three of us change the spell, the others will have to follow. Then those poor soldiers will at least have a fighting chance. Ah!'

The spell bubble began to envelop the Talish barges, and Rose could hear the cries of surprise and horror as the soldiers saw the sky change colour to an eerie cast of silvery grey. Perhaps they thought it was some strange uncanny storm.

Once the spell surrounded the ships, they should have swept them under the water, but there was a moment of stillness, as no one could bear to start such devastation. And in that moment, Miranda, Miss Fell and Rose swept in like a whirlwind, splitting the boards of the ships apart, ripping the ropes, and scattering the infantry into the freezing sea. Rose couldn't help murmuring, 'Sorry,' as her magic swirled past, but of course, she didn't know it in Talish. A sparkling white flurry of fur shot past her, as Gus gleefully joined in.

It took a horribly short time.

Rose blinked, and shivered, and opened her eyes. The fire was burning brightly, and somewhere in the depths of the house she could smell muffins toasting. Two hundred miles away, men were fighting and scrambling to get aboard the scraps of wood that were all that was left of their ships, but at Fell Hall, it was time for tea.

She shivered again, and felt her mother's rose-pink silk frock brush past her. It was ten years out of date, but still beautiful after all its years in a cedar-lined dressing room. Miranda kneeled in front of her and caught her hands. 'Don't. Think instead what might have happened if they had landed on the beaches, Rose. The Talish emperor is not merciful, and we have been at war, secretly or not, for the last fifty years. It would have been a massacre.'

'Can we go back to London now? Can we go back home?' Rose asked stiffly. She wasn't sure if it was her home any more.

Her mother smiled. 'Mr Fountain was most put out

229

when he realised that my return might disrupt your apprenticeship. He forced me to promise that I would not take you away from his house. So much so that he invited me to live there too, and assist in teaching you all.'

Rose smiled back, and then laughed out loud as she caught Freddie's face, an expression of complete horror.

Gus leaped into Rose's lap, and stared up at her mother, his eyes jewel-like slits. 'Shall we bring the peacocks with us back to London?'

Rose stroked him, and rubbed behind his ears. 'Would you rather have a peacock, or a whole fricasséed lobster?' she whispered.

Her mother nodded. 'You're a war hero, now, you know. You could probably claim a lifetime of lobster from the king.'

'There's not the same enjoyment in stalking a lobster,' Gus muttered regretfully. 'They're terribly slow. But delicious.'

Rose smiled at him, rubbing the back of her hand over the soft, silk fur beneath his ears. It felt quite normal, to be using magic to discuss expensive seafood with a cat. Far more normal than it did to be discussing *anything* with her mother. Rose still couldn't quite believe she had one. But she was starting to feel that she might rather like it. Every so often she looked up to find her mother's eyes fixed on her, and filled with a strange sort of delighted amazement. No one had ever looked at Rose that way before.

The drawing room door eased slowly open, and several maids entered with trays of tea. Bill followed them with a large platter of sandwiches, which he brought straight to Rose. He bowed briefly to Miranda and Miss Fell. 'You did it then?' he murmured to Rose, offering her a sandwich, and pretending not to see as a white paw reached over the side of the salver. 'The potted shrimp sandwiches are on the other side, miss, should you wish for one,' he added. The paw disappeared, and a sandwich disappeared from the other side.

Rose nodded. 'It worked.' She smiled at him, her eyes creasing at the corners, and a delicious feeling of excitement glowing inside her. 'And now we're going home.'

Don't miss the amazing
new series from Holly Webb

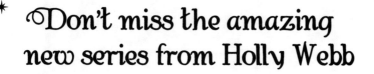

Lily

OUT NOW!

Read on for an exclusive extract of *The Magical Detectives...*

To look at, there was nothing very remarkable about Otto Spinoza. He was about average height for a boy of twelve. He had very clear blue eyes and floppy brown hair, which he was in the habit of tossing back from his forehead from time to time. His teacher at school thought he was rather quiet, but she concluded that he was merely thoughtful and left it at that.

However, there were at least two things about Otto that *were* very much out of the ordinary. The first was the fact that from as far back as he could remember, Otto had had the feeling that he was different from the other boys and girls in his school; for some reason, which he could not quite put his finger on, he simply did not belong. He didn't talk about this feeling to anyone, because he didn't want to seem rude or stuck-up. But it was always there.

The second unusual thing about Otto was the mystery of his father's death: he had died of a rare tropical disease shortly after Otto was born. So rare was this disease, that no one else in England had ever contracted it, and by the time the hospital realised what was wrong, it was too late to do anything about it. The doctors had been extremely puzzled because even in the jungles of Borneo, where the disease originated, it had only reared its ugly head a few times in the last hundred years. The conclusion they had come to was that Mr Spinoza, who was a bookseller by trade, must have been bitten by an insect that had stowed away in a crate of books he had bought at an auction the week before.

Otto had often wondered why the insect had not bitten anyone else, such as the person who put the books in the crate in the first place, or the auctioneer, but no one seemed to know the answer to this.

Otto and his mother lived in the sleepy little town of Bridlington Chawley, in an apartment above the second-hand bookshop that his mother now ran. It was not the sort of home you see featured in magazines or on television programmes.

The furniture was rickety, the carpets threadbare and the rooms all needed a coat of paint. But Otto did not mind all that. He liked living above a bookshop because he loved to read, and there were always plenty of books waiting for his attention.

Otto's mother was a dreadful worrier. When it rained, she worried that the roof might leak, when it was cold she worried that the central heating might break, and when it was warm she worried that it would not last. She worried about her health, and about her weight, about whether or not she was going to be able to pay all the bills. But most of all she worried about Otto, and in particular about what would become of him if anything should happen to her.

'They'll come round sticking their noses in, asking all sorts of questions, that's what they'll do,' she frequently complained. 'Then they'll take you away and put you in a home for orphans. There'll be no one to care for you, no one to look after you. Oh, Otto, I can't bear to think about it!'

At this point she always burst into tears and Otto was obliged to make her a cup of strong tea, and open a packet of biscuits.

Otto's mother had a great fondness for biscuits. They were the only thing that really stopped her worrying for any length of time. It was because of this that Otto was not present when one of the most extraordinary things in the history of Bridlington Chawley took place. She had sent him to the corner shop for a couple of packets of chocolate digestives. So he only discovered what had happened when he returned.

It was the first day of the summer holidays, and all the way to the shop Otto was thinking about what he would do in the weeks to come. Other children in his class went on holiday to exotic places, but there was no chance of that for Otto. Even if they could afford to go away, his mother would be far too worried to contemplate such a trip. Perhaps if his father had been alive, Otto thought to himself, things might have been different.

He was still thinking about what might have been when he arrived back home to find the door of the bookshop wide open and no sign of his mother. Surprised, he stepped into the shop. Immediately the hairs on the back of his neck stood on end and goosebumps sprang up all over his body. The air in the shop seemed to crackle with energy as though a thunderstorm might break out above the bookshelves at any moment. It made Otto quite dizzy. He took hold of a bookcase and steadied himself.

'Mum?' he called out. 'Where are you?'

There was no answer. He walked across the shop and opened the door to the stock room. But it was empty, except for the hundreds and hundreds of characters who lived within the dusty covers of the books. He could almost hear them muttering unhappily to each other, as if they, too, sensed that something was wrong.

Otto looked in the back yard in case his mother was putting out the rubbish. Then he went upstairs and checked the apartment that they both shared. There was no sign of her. But in the kitchen, stuck to the front of the refrigerator door was a set of magnetic letters that had been there ever since he was a baby. He hadn't played with them for many years. They had been rearranged into two words.

HELP ME.